CHATEAU OF THE WINDMILL

Hannah's employer, a public relations agency, has despatched her to France to handle the promotion of a Chateau which is to be converted into an hotel. However Gerrard, the son of the owner, resents the conversion, and some of the residents of the Chateau are not what they seem to be. Now she begins to find herself entangled both in a mystery that surrounds a valuable tapestry, and also a Frenchman's romantic intentions . . .

SHEILA BENTON

CHATEAU OF THE WINDMILL

Complete and Unabridged

LINFORD
Leicester

First published in Great Britain in 2006

First Linford Edition
published 2007

British Library CIP Data

Benton, Sheila
    Chateau of the Windmill.—Large print ed.—
    Linford romance library
    1. Castles—France—Fiction
    2. Love stories
    3. Large type books
    I. Title
    823.9′2 [F]

    ISBN 978–1–84617–603–6

Published by
F. A. Thorpe (Publishing)
Anstey, Leicestershire

Set by Words & Graphics Ltd.
Anstey, Leicestershire
Printed and bound in Great Britain by
T. J. International Ltd., Padstow, Cornwall

This book is printed on acid-free paper

1

As she stepped from the ferry with the other foot passengers, Hannah came to an abrupt stop. Taking a deep breath she allowed herself a moment simply to enjoy the air.

The two countries are not far apart, she thought. Just 20 miles at the narrowest part of the channel, but France and England are so different, it's as though thousands of miles separate them.

It was two years since she was last here and immediately she was caught up in the atmosphere. She smiled, thinking that here there were different smells and a lighter mood as though the trials of life were soon resolved with cheese and a bottle of wine.

Looking about her, she joined the throng going through control. As usual no-one was interested in her passport and even seemed mildly irritated that she dared to wave it at Customs.

Just a cursory glance was given before a throaty voice muttered, 'Passez, passez.' The tone of the voice telling her he'd better things to do than check her document.

Glancing around, she searched for the number of the car she'd been given. She couldn't immediately see it, but there was time enough and she was happy to take in the atmosphere and listen to the high, quick, French voices around her.

It was funny how she'd always loved France, right from school holidays through to the recent year spent working near Paris, and was happy to be back.

If Hannah was asked to describe why she had this love affair with France, she'd say she appreciated its tremendous sense of style. There was definitely an affinity with the emphasis on the social aspect of eating and drinking. Here there was no rush to clear a table and wash up, but just more wine or coffee and endless conversation. So much more relaxing for the digestion she thought wryly.

This aspect of French life coupled with the variation in the character of the regions was endlessly fascinating. She'd envied the sophistication of the Parisians, but also loved the contrasting gentleness and slow pace of life in Brittany.

She was so lost in her thought that she hadn't noticed someone approach, and jumped slightly as he spoke.

'Mademoiselle,' a short stocky man touched her arm briefly. 'Mademoiselle 'annah James?'

'Yes, er, oui,' she murmured, looking at the man and overcoming the urge to laugh at the difficulty always caused with the first letter of her name.

Fortunately he continued in good, but stilted English. 'I am the chauffeur of Madame Foultiere. I am Claude.' He looked down, 'your bags?' Then not waiting for a reply he continued, 'you follow me please,' and as he spoke, he swung the two cases up and walked ahead of her to the waiting car.

She decided to sit beside him, in order to see more of the scenery and for a while they drove in silence. The busy port with the surrounding area of pavement cafés was soon left behind and they turned on to quieter roads where Hannah was content to watch the scenery.

Realising suddenly, that she was a boring passenger and should make some effort at conversation, she turned to Claude, 'Tell me about the chateau, is it very big?' As she spoke, it suddenly dawned on her that he'd spoken English even though with a thick accent.

Even while driving, he managed a shrug. 'Not compared to many. Non, I say this is a small one, but there is much excitement, Mademoiselle, in preparation of the work you are here to do.'

She smiled and spoke a few sentences

of good French which appeared to please him. It wouldn't take long to get her tongue around the words again.

Then her excitement vanished as she thought about why she was here.

Her heart lurched as for the umpteenth time she wondered if she was up to the job. The responsibility weighed heavily and she was suddenly overcome with panic.

She had been handed this plum commission and it was the most frightening and exciting opportunity of her whole 23 years.

The public relations agency she worked for was to handle the promotion of the impressive Chateau du Moulin, which was shortly to become a hotel. The publicity was to be a package of words and pictures.

She needed to explore the area and discover the history of the building as well as taking photographs of the interior and also some of the surrounding area so that they could form a small brochure.

Her and Jack usually worked together, but this time her boss had convinced her that this would be a big leap in her career.

The agency was just taking off and work was rolling in. Jack and another assistant were needed for an even bigger job and he had trusted her to handle this one alone.

★   ★   ★

Pushing back her shoulder length fair hair she frowned.

Anyone would give their eye teeth for this opportunity, she almost spoke aloud. So why was she like a cat on hot bricks?

Her mood swung continually from delight that she had been trusted with this prestigious work to sheer fright and worry that something would go terribly wrong.

In one way, though, she mused, it was good to be here alone. She liked Jack well enough, but recently he'd made it very plain that his feelings for her were becoming more than those of a normal working relationship.

Time spent in different countries where they were continually working together and thrown in each others company during the rest of the time, could make assignments complicated.

She sighed. He was a good friend, just seven years older than herself and although she enjoyed his company there was something missing when he kissed her.

Although at twenty-three, she thought it time she fell in love, he was not for her. There was no hurry and although she'd had plenty of opportunity to meet men while she was studying, her work always came first.

Shrugging away her thoughts, she turned to the man beside her. 'I notice your English is very good?' She let the question creep into her voice, hoping to draw him out.

'Madame insists. She looks upon us as her friends because we have been there so long,' was all he said, once again with a shrug.

'Are there many people at the chateau?' she asked, trying again to keep the conversation flowing.

'Madame's son lives there most of the time. My wife, Marie, looks after the inside with help from the local village.'

★   ★   ★

After an hour, when she lost track of the route they were taking, the car turned off the road and entered a wide curving drive. Clutching her bag as though it were a life line, Hannah felt the excitement bubble up. She glanced from side to side, her eyes taking in the avenue of plane trees and then held her breath as the chateau itself came into view.

'It is beautiful, yes?' Claude noticed her expression and slowed the car.

'It is very beautiful, yes,' she replied smiling. Then gasped as they turned slightly and she saw the windmill in the background. Her eyes were drawn back to the chateau as mentally she calculated light and lenses and wondered if she would ever be able to do it justice.

The late afternoon sun caught the fairy tale turrets and bounced from the windows to drown in a small lake below a terrace.

At last she was at the Chateau of the Windmill, and it was breathtaking.

'What a hotel this will make.' She turned to Claude. 'I'm just glad I'm here to work because I couldn't possibly afford to stay here as a guest. It is so lovely they'll be able to charge the earth.' She glanced at him and noticing his confusion said gently, 'It will be very expensive.'

He nodded. 'Yes, I think that is the idea.'

She continued, 'but in another way it must be awful to own such a property and know that other people will be tramping through it. How can the owners bear the thought of this lovely place being given over as holiday accommodation for hordes of strange people. It must be very sad for them.'

Again the typical Gaelic shrug, 'It is often necessary now, Mademoiselle. The money has all gone in keeping it in repair. It has disappeared.'

They continued the slow parade along the drive, and a few minutes later she swung her slim legs from the car and followed him to the entrance.

Here a tall, dark-haired woman come towards her and held out her hand. At once Hannah felt school-girlish against the older woman whose elegant plain dress and dark chignon spoke of typical French chic.

Mentally the girl crossed her fingers. Well, that was it, she must plunge in and hope the language, from her year of work experience in the country, would not desert her. Just as she took a deep breath and arranged some words of greeting in her mind, the wind was taken out of her sails.

'My dear,' the woman held out her

hands. 'I'm so happy you could come.'

Hannah gasped. 'You're English,' she stuttered in total confusion, 'but I thought . . . ' She flushed. 'I'm so sorry, you must think me very rude, but you look so French.'

'Ah yes.' She laughed. 'Many people make the same mistake. I have developed their way of dressing, it is what comes of being married to a Frenchman for many years.'

'I was just about to practise my language.' She smiled. 'But I'm relieved you speak English.' Then knowing that something more was expected of her, added, 'I'm so happy to be here and I hope you won't be disappointed in what I do for you Madame Foultiere.'

'Disappointed?' She wrinkled her nose and Hannah immediately regretted her impulsive speech.

She must keep a careful guard on her tongue and not give away her feeling of insecurity. 'Why should we be disappointed. You are a professional, I believe. As for French, there will be

11

plenty of time to polish it up as not every one speaks English here.'

Hannah smiled and glanced around the beautifully proportioned entrance hall with its panelled walls and columns. 'It's magnificent, it will be a wonderful experience to stay here, Madame.'

'I hope you will enjoy it, apart from your work.' She hesitated, 'in a way you will be our first guest.'

'I'm sure I shall love it,' she said smiling.

'You must call me Anne,' said the other woman. Claude has already taken your cases to your room and I will show you the way.'

She led Hannah up a wide staircase and through to a room at the back of the building.

For the first time, Hannah noticed that Anne looked rather distracted and was glancing at her watch.

'I hope you will excuse me, it does seem terribly rude to go out directly you arrive but,' she checked her watch again. 'I have to pick up someone.' She smiled briefly. 'I shall not be long and perhaps you'd like to look around on your own for a while. You will be able to get the feel of the place.' She looked at the younger girl. 'Or perhaps you would prefer a rest?'

'That's perfectly all right, I shall probably look around,' Hannah replied, but thought it rather strange to be abandoned so quickly. Whoever Anne was meeting must be important or surely she would have sent Claude.

Then she realised the other woman was turning to the door and speaking again. 'If you need anything, ask Marie.' She pointed to a tray, 'there is some light refreshment if you are hungry and I'll see you before dinner.'

With that she was gone, and Hannah had the opportunity to take in her surroundings. She was in, she thought, one of the smaller bedrooms. Pretty, but at the same time quite functional. Behind a door there was a tiny ensuite bathroom which was obviously a new edition. Probably used to be a walk-in wardrobe, she mused.

On the tray there was a flask of coffee and a baguette with jam which had thoughtfully been provided. Sitting on the bed she munched appreciatively.

Feeling restless, she dusted the last crumb from her lips and decided to do as Anne suggested, and explore.

Pulling out a pair of slim fitting jeans and shirt she remembered she was in France and grinned. The shirt was discarded in favour of a fine flowing top with thick lace at the cuffs. Then clutching up her bag, she withdrew her one bottle of expensive perfume and sprayed it liberally at her throat and wrists. 'Enjoy the life of luxury while you can,' she said under her breath.

Hearing an engine start, she moved across the room and kneeling on the window seat, saw Anne in a small car, drive herself from the chateau. She was just about to turn away when she heard men's voices below her window, but out of sight. She couldn't see who it was, but the voices carried up to her and suddenly, without meaning to, she was eavesdropping.

'Madame is determined to go through with it? She will not change her mind?'

Then a second voice. 'No, and while she is occupied there will be opportunity to . . . '

The conversation drifted away and although she angled herself, trying to glimpse the men, she saw no-one. They must have been passing close to the wall of the chateau she presumed and consequently out of her view.

She bit her lip going over the conversation in her mind. Did it mean that somebody disapproved of the chateau being used as a hotel, or even worse did they disapprove of her being here.

However, thinking about things sensibly, it could also be something quite different they were discussing. Flushing, she regretted hearing the disturbing conversation even though her eavesdropping had not been deliberate. She would be better not knowing for now, she would weigh every word that was spoken.

Taking a deep breath she tried to put the unfortunate episode of the over-heard conversation from her mind. It was time to do her tour. Hesitating before leaving her room she wondered quite where to start and then perversely she grabbed a jacket and decided to look at the grounds first.

After all, she'd been travelling since early morning and in the late afternoon sun the exterior looked inviting. Some-how she knew the terraced garden, she'd glimpsed when she arrived, was only part of the setting for the beauty of the building.

For an hour she wandered, breathing in the atmosphere and working out the best view points for photographs. Now and again she stopped and wrote in a small pocket book. She wanted to get down her first impressions of the place. That way she could retain her initial enthusiasm before she became too used to it all. Piece by piece she would build up her first draft which would be a framework for her finished piece.

The formal flowerbeds had been laid out with precision, but managed to look completely natural. Trying to identify certain plants, she turned a corner and was so deep in plans and ideas that she was surprised at the sight of two men near one of the statues. As she remembered hearing the voices beneath her window she experienced a strong sense of déja-vu.

Cautiously she eyed them while she debated what to do. Suddenly she felt very alone, should she address them or turn and walk another way and so avoid the encounter altogether.

They could, she supposed, be work-men and then she changed her mind. Although casually dressed they both had an air of authority which made her think otherwise. She wondered what to do, in two minds whether to walk to the lake she had glimpsed in the distance but it appeared to be too far.

For a moment she was faintly embarrassed and thought she might turn and walk in the direction of the wrought iron gates as though she was leaving the grounds. Presumably the men were French, so should she speak or just smile and walk on, should she perhaps even introduce herself?

Perhaps they would think she was trespassing. She giggled softly, how would she introduce herself? Did Madame Foultiere want people to know why she was here?

2

However, as she neared the men, the decision was taken out of her hands.

'Bonjour Mademoiselle,' the taller one greeted her and then continued in English. 'I expect you are Hannah James,' he held out his hand. 'I am Gerrard Foultiere and this is Pierre Almonde.'

So Madame had a son, well there was nothing unusual about that although it was odd she hadn't mentioned his presence before she left. She took his hand and looked up at a rather long face with alert blue eyes under dark brows.

Murmuring a greeting she knew she had heard the deep timbre of his voice before from the window in her room.

She turned to the other man but when he spoke, his voice was also deep. It could have been either of them or both, but in any case it wasn't really her concern.

'But why are you alone, where is my mother?' Gerrard questioned.

When she told him that his mother had to rush away, his expression grew angry.

'Robert,' he said, just the one word but there was plenty of meaning in it.

Suddenly he smiled and said, 'In the absence of my mother we will show you the grounds,' and as though the meeting was arranged, the two men escorted her along several more paths, chatting generally and answering her questions, both happy to place their knowledge at her disposal.

Pierre was on easy terms with the son of the house, so she supposed he was a friend. Certainly nothing was said as to his position here. The attentions of the young men, both of similar appearance with their dark hair and slim build made her feel extremely feminine. Now she was ridiculously pleased she'd obeyed her instinct and paid so much attention to her dress.

As the men spoke to each other, her thoughts returned to her eavesdropping. Although one voice was obviously English and the other charmingly accented, she was sure it was the same men. At the time she hadn't noticed the accent but she was convinced they were the two she'd heard beneath her room.

Why was she dwelling on the episode and determinedly, putting it from her mind, gave herself up to the enjoyment of their attentions.

Smiling at how good it made her feel when they both put a hand out to help her over an uneven path. When at last, the inspection was complete, they walked with her up the steps to the entrance.

It was here that she couldn't resist stroking the old stone, murmuring, 'beautifully cut from the loveliest of stone.'

Gerrard placed a hand under her arm and led her into the hall. 'Let me show you around in the absence of my mother,' he said formally. Then he grinned, 'I'm sure she would have asked me had I been in earlier, but I appear to have just missed her.'

Pierre seemed reluctant to go. After a few minutes conversation he gave her a charming smile with that special some-thing in his dark eyes, typical of Frenchmen and drifted away.

She was left with Gerrard who led her decisively by the hand from room to room. Time sped as he painstakingly described each one and its contents as though she were on an official guided tour. He was so knowledgeable and appreciative of the furnishings and pictures that she decided he must be an artist.

'These old places are usually built on high ground with masses of space around them which gives the most amazing light.'

'I knew it,' she exclaimed. 'You're an artist.'

He shook his head. 'No talent I'm afraid. After a term at art school I settled for a change of course into interior design.' He smiled down at her a little sadly. 'I'm not happy about some of the things going into store.' He gestured to a set of upholstered chairs. 'These for instance. They belong here. Imagine them under wraps in a stuffy warehouse.'

'Yes,' she murmured. 'I agree they should be seen.' She studied the rich fabric, 'but really,' she continued more practically. 'When there are hotel guests, they are too beautiful to be put to everyday use by people staying here.' She hesitated. 'I wonder if they should be in the photographs? I should hate to mention them in the brochure and then find that they are in storage.'

Suddenly his face closed down. 'Hotel, of course I'm forgetting.' He looked at her, 'and you are part of this, you are here for the brochure.' His smile disappeared making him look suddenly older and quite angry.

Heavens, she thought, I hope he isn't going to take his ill temper out on me because I am here to work on the P.R. for the hotel. Having previously put his age at about twenty-five, she now glanced at his drawn brows and thought him to be nearer thirty.

Then as quickly as it left, his good humour returned as they gazed together through a window and over the beautiful grounds. 'Of course I see my mother's point of view, it takes an army of men just to keep the gardens in order without the inside. I sometimes wonder how she knows every one who works here.' Then he lightly touched her arm to continue their progress.

The ballroom was splendid and for a moment she could hear an old fashioned minuet and almost see figures dancing in wigs and gowns. 'What will you use this for?' She frowned. 'Will you hold dances?'

Again there was that shuttered look as he uttered the one word, 'No.'

It was on an upper landing that she saw the tapestry and she stopped abruptly, her hand going up instinctively to touch it and then falling away again. 'It's magnificent,' she moved closer, 'this is amazing, woven of course and the colours are wonderful. It must be very valuable.' She peered even closer. 'It certainly looks it.'

'Very,' he said abruptly, 'and there are people who would like to get their hands on it.'

Deciding to ignore his comment, she studied it intently. 'It reminds me of work from the Gobelins Workshop.' She shook her head. 'Or is it Brussels, I'm not sure.'

'For someone in public relations you seem to have a lot of general art knowledge.' He frowned. 'You are the P.R. person, I take it. I haven't made an awful blunder have I.'

Laughing she shook her head. 'No, you haven't, but I split my studies in the last year and included Art History.' She grinned feeling happier. 'So although I know a little about many aspects of art, I am certainly not expert about anything.'

He joined her laughter. 'Well, you could have fooled me, you are certainly a most knowledgeable young woman.' His blue eyes swept over her, 'as well as a very attractive one.'

She had discarded her jacket and he now studied her openly, 'with the lace at your wrists and the velvet ribbon in your hair, you look as though you belong here.' His glance took in her jeans, 'apart from those of course.' He laughed and she joined him.

Hannah was pleased out of all proportion that this young man found her attractive. It warmed her and the fears about the assignment slipped away. Perversely, she was now pleased that she'd come alone without Jack. But, she pulled herself up short, she was here to work, not to have her head turned by the son of the woman who was paying for her services.

Abruptly he changed the subject. 'Did my mother mention where she was going?'

'Just to meet someone, I believe. She

said she wouldn't be away very long.' She wanted to know more about the family so she asked, 'Is your father around or are there any other members of the family staying here?'

'My father died fairly recently,' he stated flatly, 'and I am the only one.'

'So the chateau belongs to both you and your mother,' she asked as she remembered the complexity of the French inheritance laws.

'No,' the word dropped into the silence. It was several seconds before he spoke again. 'The chateau belongs entirely to my mother. It was bought by her. In the beginning she had the money, you see. But she loved the place and unwisely poured all her money into it.'

Flushing, Hannah spoke quickly. 'I'm so sorry, I didn't mean to pry. I was just so interested in the place and I . . . '

'It's all right. You just touched on a rather sore subject that's all.'

At that moment there was the sound of an approaching car and turning to the window they watched Anne neatly park the small Renault.

She alighted in an easy, elegant movement which Hannah wryly envied. From the passenger side a tall, grey-haired man got out and together, looking on the friendliest of terms, they walked to the entrance of the chateau.

'I thought it was him,' Gerrard said under his breath and Hannah just caught the words, but the expression of distaste in his face was so obvious that once again she wondered what was going on here. 'Damned Americans should stay in their own country. No history of their own so they try to filch other peoples.'

Hannah stared, surprised and intrigued, she would love to ask more, but Gerrard's face was dark and he appeared to have forgotten her presence entirely.

She took the opportunity to study him, noting the thickness of his dark brows which were now drawn tightly together. He was tall for a Frenchman, she thought and then remembered he was part English and Anne was a tall woman.

Even so, he must be a little over six foot and there was just the slightest resemblance to Pierre. Maybe they were related in some way. She moved slightly and obviously broke his train of thought, even so when he left the window, he seemed surprised to see her.

Trying to cover the awkward moment, she thanked him for allowing her to take up his time and for showing her around. 'What time is dinner?' she asked.

'We usually have an aperitif about 7.45 and go in about 8 o'clock.'

A sudden thought struck her. 'Do you er . . . dress?' She asked knowing that she had not really brought anything suitable.

'Not really,' he glanced at her long legs, 'although Mother does not like trousers at the table.'

She flushed again, wondering if he

thought her completely gauche and uncivilised. 'I wasn't intending to come to the table in jeans,' she said rather haughtily and grinned.

'I'll see you at dinner, no doubt,' and he was walking away without another glance, leaving her standing in the middle of the room.

With some difficulty she found the way back to her own room to discover that in her absence someone had unpacked her clothes and they were neatly in the wardrobe and drawers.

What a life, she grinned to herself. I could get used to this very easily. Well, enjoy it tonight because tomorrow there is work to be done.

Later, pulling open the wardrobe door, she studied the meagre contents. Not wanting to overload her two small cases, she hadn't brought a lot. There'd been enough to carry with all her work equipment without worrying about extra clothes.

However, she pulled out a black full skirt which doubled nicely for day or dressed up for evening wear. She topped it with a cream silk blouse and added an old fashioned gold locket which had been a present from her grandmother.

She wondered also if Madame's friend would be joining them and if so, how would Gerrard behave. It could be a fascinating meal because when Gerrard had seen the man from the window he'd obviously not been at all pleased.

She'd sensed a strong dislike of the older man and if it was returned then her first dinner at the chateau could be a stormy one. There was something odd going on here. Her intuition was working overtime and she could feel the undercurrents surging with strong emotions.

Then she remembered Anne, for all her protestations of being English, there was a French aura about her that would put paid to any unpleasantness at her table, Hannah was sure. The meal would be relaxed and pleasant and any undercurrents would be kept firmly under control.

Nevertheless it would be interesting to see who would be there and how they would behave. Taking a deep breath she pushed open the door and entered the room.

★   ★   ★

At first glance it appeared full of people, and she stood in the doorway for a moment, quiet and unnoticed. As her eyes swept over everyone, she saw that there was really only five others here. Anne and the older man, who was presumably her friend, were sitting close together, apart from the rest.

The group standing a little away from Anne, consisted of two men and a girl. The men were Gerrard and Pierre, but between them stood a tiny, dark-haired girl who looked so typically French, she fitted into the room as a hand into the right size glove.

Everything about the girl was perfect.

From her slim black dress to her long dark hair, which was a perfect foil for her olive skin and almost black eyes.

Then she noticed the girl's hand on Gerrard's dark sleeve and experienced a wave of sudden jealousy. Her face flushed guiltily as though every person in the room knew what she was thinking.

Instinctively she put up a nervous hand to touch her own hair and suddenly her confidence drained away. How ordinary and English I must look, she thought to herself as she gazed with envy at the chic of the other girl.

She felt so completely out of place that she just wanted to run away. For one moment she even considered fleeing back home. How she must lack presence for no-one had even noticed she was standing there.

Then the spell was broken as Anne rose, holding out her hand. 'Hannah, my dear, how pretty you look.' She turned and gestured to the rest of the room. 'A perfect English rose.'

That says it all, thought Hannah grimly. How I'd like to be mysterious and sophisticated, and her joy in being in her beloved France started to slide away. Now she felt dowdy and old fashioned in her full skirt with the locket at her throat.

Her outfit was all wrong. It simply didn't fit in with her surroundings, so perhaps tomorrow she should buy some more suitable clothes. Then gritting her teeth, she pushed the stupid ideas back where they belonged. She must keep her mind on work. That was the sole reason she was here and she'd better remember it.

Somehow, she had a drink in her hand and she sipped the cloudy Pernod wishing for once there was some good dry sherry. Anne was clearly pleased to see her and chatted companionably, obviously trying to make up for her previous neglect.

Unnoticed, the older man had joined them and as they were introduced, Hannah looked up into the friendliest face she'd ever seen. It was a lived-in face with grey eyes framed with short crinkly lines fanning out at the sides. His smiling mouth was wide and genuine as he took both her hands in a warm clasp.

'I'm Robert, from America and we visitors must stick together,' he said in a low conspiratorial voice and she felt the warmth of his personality flow through her. It was as though he'd guessed her thoughts and was trying to reassure her.

Then Anne was moving forward towards the group of young people and momentarily Hannah panicked again.

Where would she fit in, not surely with these three sophisticated young people and not with Anne and Robert whom she guessed would like to be left alone.

3

A wonderful thing happened, Gerrard smiled and appeared to be pleased to see her. Her confidence rose until she heard him say, 'Here she is,' and he turned to the other young woman. 'It'll be nice for you to have another girl around.' Annick was Pierre's sister, and looking at them standing together, she could see the family resemblance.

Annick's cool, ''allo,' did nothing to put Hannah at ease and her hand felt large as it closed around the dainty fingers of the French girl. Once more she took refuge in her drink and now sipped gratefully, enjoying the warmth and relaxation that spread along her veins.

Annick didn't seem particularly pleased to meet her and as she listened to their conversation she tried to fit each one into a place. It appeared that

Annick worked for Gerrard in his business and they appeared to be very close.

Pierre was quite the opposite and made no secret of the fact that he was delighted to see her and asked how she'd enjoyed the tour of the house.

Annick, however, did not possess the easy friendly manner of her brother and her eyes when she looked at Hannah were resentful and cold.

Why should she resent me? Hannah tried to work out what was happening. It was one intrigue after another, but then she saw the other girl touch Gerrard on the hand and look up into his face, and she knew.

Good heavens, she thought, her confidence soaring, she thinks I'm a rival. What a fool I was to feel so inadequate when it's obvious she's worried about me. She grinned and hugging the thought to herself, tossed back her drink and drifted with the others into dinner.

Fortunately she was placed beside

Robert, and as they waded through several courses, he kept her amused with stories about the gallery he owned. 'Although I sell pictures,' he admitted, 'I'm very interested in art and antiques generally. There's plenty of money to be made if you know what you're looking for.'

For a moment, Hannah was worried, thinking that one moment she had him neatly filed into a box marked nice, and now he was talking about making big money selling treasures. Goodness, the idea horrified her, surely he hadn't got the beautiful pieces of the chateau in mind.

Then she looked at his face and knew he was utterly genuine. However, only half her attention was on him. Part of her watched the rest of the table. It appeared that Anne and Pierre had a lot to talk about, their voices were low and serious.

Unashamedly, Hannah strained her ears to hear without appearing to do so. Now and again she caught snatches of conversation, but by far the biggest competitor for her attention was the performance of Annick. Because, a performance it certainly was. Frequently she laughed, touching Gerrard in some way and looking into his eyes. Then as she saw Gerrard smile and bend towards the girl, she felt a cold hand around her heart.

That was ridiculous, she'd only just met the man, and working her way through the delicious courses, she tried to concentrate on Robert whose kindness deserved her full attention.

'What did you think of the tapestry?' he asked with a smile. 'Isn't it the most wonderful thing you've ever seen?'

As she started to reply she was aware of an abrupt silence opposite her. Gerrard was no longer talking to Annick, but his whole attention was concentrated on Robert.

'Er . . . ' for a moment Hannah missed the thread of conversation, then pulled herself together quickly. 'It's wonderful. I couldn't quite put a name to it, I'd need to look at a reference book, but I'm sure it's terribly valuable.' She frowned as she continued, 'I'm no expert, but I would put it at sometime during the seventeen-hundreds.' Then impulsively she asked, 'What will happen to it when the hotel is opened for business?'

Now everyone had stopped talking and were looking at her and Robert. It was like a tableau, frozen in time, she thought as her mind wrestled with trying to keep up her side of the conversation and wonder why it was of such interest to the rest of the party.

Robert shrugged. 'It ought to go into safe-keeping, I keep telling Anne, but,' he hesitated, 'on the other hand, a thing like that should be on show, not hidden away. People should have a chance to enjoy it.'

'Where would you suggest it was shown?'

'Oh,' he answered casually, 'somewhere safe but accessible to people, like a museum.'

'Or a gallery?' Gerrard had obviously

been listening and broke in coldly, giving the word a special emphasis.

Anne said quickly, 'It is nice to know how much Hannah appreciates our treasures, Gerrard. I'm sure it will make all the difference to her report.'

Hannah felt quite warm. There was something odd going on here and her intuition was working overtime. What a strange family she was to work with. Gerrard obviously disliked Robert, she was sure of that now, and there had been other small hints during the short time she'd been here.

But for the moment the atmosphere had relaxed, and as the next course arrived the conversation became more general and she let it drift around her.

Hannah eyed her tomato salad with pleasure and found her mind wandering back to earlier that afternoon. When she'd admired the tapestry, Gerrard had become abrupt and almost rude. He had the same attitude now and his inference had been almost an insult to Robert.

Whatever was going on here it had something to do with the tapestry and its future. Somehow, Robert, however genuine he seemed, was looked upon with suspicion by Gerrard. What could possibly be worrying him to such an extent that he risked rudeness at the dinner table.

Robert drew her attention to her empty glass and Hannah shook her head smiling and saying that she didn't really drink very much.

'You mustn't monopolise our lady visitor.' Gerrard looked across at them coldly.

All at once Hannah was overcome with guilt. Should she have spoken so much and so freely to Robert? Had she given offence to Anne? But no, Anne was back in conversation with Pierre. It was Gerrard who was irritated and somehow in referring to her as, 'our lady visitor', had put her well outside the circle at the table.

Her joy in the lovely meal and surroundings evaporated and once more she knew she was an outsider and just here to do a job.

They sat at the dining table until midnight drinking wine and endless coffee. As time wore on, Hannah felt more and more an outsider. How she longed to have her coffee with her legs tucked up on a deep sofa at home, but this was France and she must make an effort to fit in.

At last reprieve came, and almost stumbling up the stairs she didn't notice the beauty of the chateau. But tired as she was, she lay for a long time going over all the events of her very busy day. It's the travel, new place, different people and different ways, she told herself.

⋆ ⋆ ⋆

Next morning, her spirits were revived and her energy levels were back to normal, but she needed fresh air and her own company to put her thoughts in order. She must first have a long talk with Anne and then maybe there would be time for herself.

But Anne obviously had arrangements and said that she regretted there would not be time that day to go over things with Hannah.

In a way she was relieved because now she could leave the glamour and the strained atmosphere within the chateau.

'Is it far to the village?' she asked Anne shortly after breakfast. A breakfast which the two women had shared. Gerrard had already left for his business and Robert was sleeping off his jetlag. Annick and Pierre weren't mentioned.

'Do you ride?' asked Anne.

'I like horses but haven't really had much opportunity to learn to ride.'

'No,' the older woman laughed. 'Actually I mean a bicycle because I have an old bike in one of the garages. It would save you a three mile walk.'

By the time she'd collected a small camera, tape recorder and notebook, the cycle was propped against the beautiful façade of the building. It looked totally out of place with its upright frame and large front basket and Hannah grinned as she swung her bag over her back and set off following Anne's directions.

On each side of the road the fields were gently undulating and she passed cream-coloured villas with deep coffee coloured shutters and large wooden gates. How lovely to own one of those for a holiday place, she thought as she pedalled idly along on her way to the village.

Once there, it was amazingly quiet with a wide main street that was without traffic. Not like the busy roads at home, she thought. Where is everyone, was her next thought for the place seemed largely deserted.

She dismounted at the church and pushed the bike around to the village square. Trees lined the area on three sides and she looked eagerly at the tables outside a small café.

Just a coffee she promised herself,

after all she had cycled here and was in need of a drink. Then she would unload her small recorder and camera and start work.

She turned the bike in the direction of the café. 'I recognise that old thing.' She jumped at the voice near her shoulder. 'What are you doing here? I thought you'd be exploring the chateau.'

Her face grew warm while she tried to work out whether or not Gerrard was accusing her of not doing her job.

Smiling at him, she decided to assume it was just a casual comment. 'Oh we always like to explore the neighbouring villages. It interests people who are on holiday and we like to describe the surroundings. In this instance it will help present a whole picture of the chateau so it's not just an unrelated building, but in its right setting. For however beautiful, everything needs a background.'

He smiled at her earnest face. 'Come and have coffee with me and tell me your first impressions.'

The invitation was quite a relief, for obviously he wasn't worried about her wasting time. He took the bike from her and pushed it to the side of the tables. He was obviously well known and coffee arrived almost as they sat down.

There was something wonderful about the smell of coffee, especially in France, she decided and over the rim of her cup she caught his eyes looking into her own and found she couldn't look away.

His were startlingly blue against his dark hair and then she grinned thinking that perhaps he was surprised at her own dark hazel eyes against the fairness of her hair.

Their gazes were locked across the table and a delightful frisson of excitement ran through her before common sense asserted itself. This wasn't the time to be involved with a man, certainly not on this assignment which was so important to her. It wasn't the time, not now when her career had taken such an upward turn.

To break the spell, she gulped down some hot coffee and spluttered and choked in an undignified manner.

He rubbed her back which made things worse because she found his touch affected her even more than his gaze.

Hastily she finished her drink, and gathering up her bag said, 'I must get on. I want to get a feel for the village,' and as she left the table he was smiling as though he knew why she was leaving.

'I could give you a lift back,' he eyed the bike. 'I'm sure we could get that thing in the boot.'

It was tempting to spend more time with him, but resolutely she grabbed the handlebars and after thanking him for coffee, pushed the bike around the square until she came to the fountain.

On a convenient bench she sat down and tried to put her thoughts in order. She must put Gerrard out of her mind and concentrate on the job.

She picked up the small recorder and

looking round, slowly spoke her impressions of the village into it. After taking a few pictures with her digital camera she set off to wander around the few little shops.

It was in these that she practised her French and was quite pleased with her efforts. It was incredible that everyone at the chateau, including the chauffeur, spoke English to some degree.

At lunch time she returned to the café for another coffee and baguette to give her the energy for the ride back.

★   ★   ★

It was late afternoon when she returned to the chateau, and going directly to her room she opened her laptop and typed in her notes from the morning. It was a habit of hers to do this rather than wait until the next day when the memories were not quite so sharp.

After a shower and change of clothes, she wandered to the gallery to gaze again at the tapestry. And that was where Robert found her. Staring with a rapt expression and looking taller in her black high heeled sandals and calf length black slim dress.

She started at the sound of his voice. 'It looks as though we foreigners have a great interest in this wonderful specimen.'

'It should have a signature, but I can't make one out, I think there is a bit of damage in this corner.' She squinted at the corner. 'What do you think Robert, do you recognise the work?'

And Gerrard saw them there, talking earnestly and stood for a time watching them. He rocked slightly on his heels with a thoughtful expression in his eyes and his brows drew together. The two were so engrossed in their conversation that they didn't see him and he walked quietly away.

Several times during the next couple of days, she noticed Robert looking at the tapestry. In fact, if he wasn't with Anne, that's where he would be with an old reference book, comparing the two.

Hannah was now on such friendly terms with the American that she started to tease him. 'Does Anne know she has a rival for your affection,' she said impulsively one morning and then wondered if she'd overstepped the mark.

But he smiled and said, 'Two women in my life, but one will have to go.'

What a strange comment, she thought, and later Gerrard asked her if Robert had discussed the tapestry with her.

'Well I know he likes it, loves it perhaps, but it is so very beautiful that everyone must love it.' She shrugged her shoulders. 'Well it's probably way out of my price range so I won't be making any offers for it.' It was just a quick throwaway remark, but Gerrard took it seriously.

'Have you or Robert discussed its value?'

She bit her lip and wished she could take back her comment. She really must be more careful and think before she spoke. 'Of course, we haven't. We just form a mutual admiration society for it.' She hesitated and then had to ask, 'Is it terribly valuable?'

'The ridiculous thing is that we don't know. These things can be worth hundreds or many thousands. We could of course, have it valued, but as it was one of the last things my father bought, we decided to leave it here and enjoy it.' He paused. 'Mother, of course, would like to leave it here. But Robert, I wonder if he . . . ' and then stopped abruptly.

She laid a light hand on his arm. 'Is something worrying you Gerrard?

'Will you come out to dinner with me tonight, Hannah. I'd like to talk to you about something,' he hesitated, 'but I'd like you to have dinner with me anyway.'

★   ★   ★

She dressed carefully that evening in a deep blue skirt with a toning blouse. An old necklace which had belonged to a great aunt gleamed golden at her throat.

All my jewellery, she grinned ruefully, is second hand, but it's good quality. She brushed her hair and let it flow loosely to her shoulders.

Standing back from the mirror, she surveyed herself and knew she looked good, and later Gerrard's eyes across the table told her that he thought so too.

The wine was poured and the first course on the table when she said, 'What did you want to speak to me about, Gerrard?'

He looked as though he wasn't going to answer and then said quickly, 'This is obviously in confidence, but it's Robert. I know my mother thinks a lot of him and I want her to be happy but . . . '

'But . . . ' She prompted frowning. She wasn't sure that she liked the direction the conversation was taking.

'He's developing such an interest in the contents of the chateau and especially the tapestry.'

'Well, I don't think that's unusual. Everyone is interested in lovely things. I'm always gazing at the tapestry as well. I'm just an amateur, but Robert has a great appreciation of art and he often tells me about some of the things he has in his gallery.'

'I just wonder if it is my mother or the tapestry that interests him the most.'

'Gerrard,' she sat back shocked. 'I would say he's very fond of Anne and they are so happy together.'

'Oh, I don't want to go on about it and ruin our evening but, well, I hate to ask, but if you notice anything suspicious about him, will you let me know.'

She leaned slightly forward, her eyes troubled. 'I won't spy for you, Gerrard. I have my job to do and I'm virtually a guest here myself. I couldn't consider it because it just wouldn't be right. But,' she looked directly at him. 'If I happen to notice anything strange, I'll mention it to you but, it will have to be something serious or suspicious.'

'Thank you,' he said simply. 'I appreciate that and I know I'm asking a lot but let's forget it now and enjoy our evening.'

It would have been easy after their conversation to let it spoil the evening and for a time Hannah was disappointed. She'd thought Gerrard genuinely wanted her company, but it seemed he wanted her to report to him about Robert.

Then her mood lifted as their conversation swung to other subjects. She told him she was an only child and had longed for a brother or sister. He said that he was on his own too and they discussed the advantages and disadvantages of the only child state.

'I loved being the only one as a child,' she said honestly, 'but now I'm older, I really envy my friends who have siblings. They must be much more emotionally secure than I often feel.'

He covered her hand across the table. 'But you will marry and raise your own family and then those feelings of insecurity will fade.'

'Perhaps you're right.' She loved the feel of his hand over hers and mentally debated on whether she should leave it there and let him know that she enjoyed his touch. She could also withdraw her fingers and leave him guessing. As it happened the waiter approached their table again and needed the space, so the problem was solved.

The discussion turned to swapping information about themselves, and as she listened to his deep voice telling her about his business, she found she was totally absorbed by his voice, his eyes and his long tanned fingers. She felt utterly mesmerised by the man.

'What's happening to your business at the moment?' she asked dragging her mind back to the present.

'Well, I have an assistant and she's overseeing a couple of clients for me while I help sort things out here. Of course, it is only an hour on the train to Paris so I can be on the spot if there are any problems.

'Annick is invaluable to my business. We are a small organisation and I rely on her a lot.'

Hannah conjured up a picture of Gerrard and the dainty French girl working together, and then pushed it from her mind. She had no right to this feeling of jealousy creeping into her mind.

They lingered over coffee and then drove back through the moonlit countryside.

However, when they returned there was no time for even the tiniest spot of romance, because several of the others were still up and Gerrard joined them for a last drink before bedtime.

Hannah, however, thanked him for the evening and made her way to her room. Even when she was in bed, her mind was full of Gerrard. What would it be like to have his arms about her. His cheek against hers and then his lips pressing her own. Reluctantly she dragged her mind back to the present and work.

How glad she was that she was alone and no-one could read her mind. Nevertheless she felt her face become suddenly warm and her lips dry.

4

Anne, are you busy this morning?' Hannah asked and then sensing that the older woman was about to say she was occupied again, continued, 'I really would like to ask you a few questions about the chateau and how long you have owned it.'

'I don't know what Robert has in mind for us today.'

It was obvious to Hannah that Anne's mind was definitely on other things this morning.

Knowing she had to interview the older woman, she continued, 'I've made a schedule, perhaps you'd like to glance at it if you have time.'

Anne shrugged and Hannah thought she seemed quite disinterested. 'Perhaps you could persuade Gerrard to go over it with you. He understands that sort of thing more than me and he has more time.'

How could Gerrard have more time when he was also running a business in Paris? As nice as she found Anne, it was obvious that the older woman was not very interested in the work which Hannah was doing. Her main interest at the moment was not in the chateau, but in Robert.

Hannah was at her most persuasive and smiled gently at Anne. 'Look, it will only take a couple of hours.' She laughed gently. 'You're really my boss so you should keep a check on me. Of course I'll show you everything when it's complete so you'll have the opportunity to make alterations before it goes to print. But I'd like to know that we're on the same wavelength where the chateau is concerned.'

Still Anne hesitated and then her expression changed. 'Of course, my dear.' She laughed. 'What must you think of me. Of course you must do your job properly and I must make myself available to you.'

Hannah hadn't realised how tense she'd been until she felt her shoulders relax. Now she smiled with relief. At least she would get somewhere with Anne today.

'We'll use my private sitting-room, but first we'll pour some more coffee and take it with us.'

The two women sat either side of Anne's desk in her charming sitting-room with the early morning sun shining through the gold drapes. Hannah looked around appreciatively. 'The one thing I won't need any advice about is the absolute beauty of this place.'

Anne smiled. 'Yes, it is a beautiful place. I should be sorry to leave it.' She looked thoughtful. 'Yes, it will be very difficult.'

'But you'll stay, won't you, when it is a hotel?'

Anne didn't answer, but just sipped her coffee, then with a complete change of mood said, 'Ask me whatever you like. I . . . er, I . . . feel I've been a little off-hand since you arrived, but so many pressures, you understand.'

'That's all right. I hadn't noticed, so don't worry.' Hannah wanted to move on and not get too involved with the occupants of the house and keep the golden rule of distancing herself from them. However, she wasn't doing too well with her feelings for Gerrard.

She couldn't begin to understand the way she felt about him. Really he was one of her employers and she should want to do her best to please him. But pleasing him had assumed extra proportions for now she was eager to please him and to have him smile at her. The poor thing that she was, she wanted his approval.

'Hannah?' Anne's dark eyebrows were raised.

'Sorry, I was miles away.' She tried to cover her confusion, aware that she wasn't being very professional, just wasting time daydreaming when she'd eventually got Anne to give her some time. 'It must be this place,' she looked around the room again, 'it has such an atmosphere.' She switched on her recorder. 'Do you mind?' she questioned.

Anne shook her head.

'How long have you and your family lived here?'

Anne spoke well and with little prompting. 'I have been here all my married life and Gerrard was born here.'

'But now you want to turn it into something other than a family home?' She looked at Anne and smiled gently. 'That must be very difficult for you?'

'Yes, but of course it's money that's the problem.' She ran her hand over her hair and sat back. 'Since my husband died, it's been difficult.' She smiled, remembering. 'He had the knack of making money. His quick mind always took advantage of every opportunity.'

'What did he do?'

'Oh,' Anne's hands fluttered vaguely. 'He bought things and sold them at a profit, that sort of thing.'

Anne seemed not to want to go into details and Hannah decided not to ask any more questions just in case some of his work was slightly on the wrong side of the law. What a strange thing to think and she had no reason for that thought to come into her mind.

'But,' continued Anne, 'he liked lovely things and sometimes he kept what he bought, things like the set of chairs and the tapestry in the gallery, for instance.'

Hannah drew in her breath and leaned forward. 'It is just so beautiful. I've looked at it a few times. The weaving is so thick and the colours so rich. It must be priceless.'

'I don't know, my dear. He died shortly after he acquired it and since then we have been so worried about maintaining this place and deciding what to do that no-one has looked at it any further.'

'So what will you do with the furnishings when it is a hotel?'

She shook her head wearily. 'I don't

know. Gerrard doesn't want any hotel guests using them. He's worried that they won't be appreciated and treated with consideration.'

'Well, I must say I agree with him,' but of course she wasn't there to put her opinions forward and she turned to Anne again. 'I'm sorry to have to ask you these details. It must be painful for you but I need the information for the write-up I'm working on.' Then she grinned, 'We'll have to advertise it as an artists' retreat so we get the right type of people.' And even as she made the throwaway comment, a germ of an idea settled at the back of her mind.

⋆ ⋆ ⋆

The couple of hours dragged into over three and they'd just finished their talk when Marie told them lunch was ready.

Today it was served in the big kitchen and they ate simply with none of the elegance of their evening dining.

'You can ask me any more queries

65

while we eat,' said Anne.

Robert joined them, and when Hannah asked if Anne would be overseeing the running of the hotel herself, the older woman glanced at Robert and flushed. 'My plans are undecided at the moment which is why Pierre is spending time here. He has qualifications in hotel management and may leave his present job to join us.'

'And Gerrard? I just wondered if there would be a family member here at all times.' She must try not to appear too interested in Gerrard.

'You probably know by now that he hates the idea of it being a hotel. No-one knows what Gerrard will do.' She pushed her plate away as though it was too much trouble to eat. 'He would hate it even more if we had to sell but he has his own business, and of course there is Annick.'

'Annick?'

'Sometimes I wonder if she is more than Pierre's sister to him. I'm sure she's very fond of him. I can tell by her attitude. I think mothers always know, don't you?'

'I wouldn't know about that,' Hannah laughed, and looked away hoping the hot coffee would account for her flushed cheeks. She must be very careful not to rouse any suspicions, for clearly Anne was as sharp as anything where her son was concerned.

Crossing the hall shortly after lunch she nearly bumped into Pierre. 'Slow down,' he teased. 'You can't be that busy or do you always rush around like this?'

'Only when I'm in France,' she answered laughing.

'Have you walked to the windmill yet?' he asked.

'No, not yet, I haven't really had the time.'

'Are you free this afternoon?' Then without waiting for a reply continued, 'Shall we go now,' he asked. 'I am free for the afternoon.'

He didn't bother to ask if it was

convenient for her and she opened her mouth to say no, and then nodded her agreement.

As they set off down the drive to the gates, Pierre explained that although it was called the Chateau of the Windmill, it wasn't exactly in the grounds.

'I thought it was, because I can see the large sails clearly from the upper gallery.'

'That's because they have their covers on at the moment and so they look bigger, but it's not far.'

They walked companionably in silence and then she realised she could ask Pierre questions about the conversion to a hotel, especially if he was going to be involved.

'I hear you may be involved in the running of the hotel, Pierre?'

'Anne has spoken to me about this, but Gerrard, as you no doubt know, is not happy with the idea.'

'It does seem as though it will go ahead, though, or I shouldn't be here. Who will your clients be, what type of people are you aiming at?'

His brows drew together. 'They will have to have money. It will not be, as you say in English, 'cheap' to stay here.'

'No,' she agreed. 'I can understand that.'

'Maybe American, English, German,' he grinned, 'as long as they have money.'

'How about all the antiques, which must be valuable?'

'But,' his shrug was typically Gaelic, 'either Gerrard must come to terms with them being left out for use or they could go into store.'

'I don't think either would appeal to him.'

'Yes, he is more emotionally tied to the place than even Anne. She seems to be able to cope with the change, but she, of course, has Robert.'

The conversation came to an abrupt close as they stood in front of the windmill and gazed at the enormity of the sails now they were close to them.

'It's very old, but has been working

until recently. Do you want to look inside?'

Hannah approached the interior with enthusiasm, as they were let in by a small, elderly Frenchman. But once inside Pierre seemed to think it was necessary to place a hand under her elbow and then take her hand as he guided her around the machinery.

Even on the stroll back he still held her hand and every now and then caressed her palm with his thumb.

He's coming on a bit strong, she thought, but did it really matter. It was pleasant to be with a man who enjoyed her company and wanted to hold her hand.

He was extremely good-looking and his charming accented English only added to his charm. Maybe she should concentrate on Pierre and put Gerrard out of her mind. But she'd already resolved not to get involved with anyone during the job and knew she could fend off any advances from him. Now if it was Gerrard, then that would be a different matter.

'Have you heard about the village dance tomorrow night?'

'No,' she turned to him, 'I haven't.'

'Ah, it is something you will enjoy. We must all go.'

'All?'

'Yes, you, me, Annick and Gerrard. I don't suppose Anne and Robert will bother.'

She didn't like the sound of that pairing at all, but supposed she couldn't expect Pierre to partner his sister. 'But where,' she suddenly exclaimed. 'I borrowed Anne's bike and made quite a tour of the village and I didn't see a hall or anywhere suitable for a dance.'

'Hall?' He puzzled and then laughed. 'But this is France, not England. The weather it is good and we have the dance outside in the village square and nearly everyone will be there.'

'But what about music and all that stuff?'

Pierre laughed.

'It is all arranged and you will see.'

When they reached the chateau, they separated and Hannah went in search of Anne. 'Pierre suggested that we go to the village dance tomorrow. He said we dance in the street. What shall I wear? I've really no idea.'

Anne looked at the younger girl and thought how different and more relaxed she looked from the one who interviewed her this morning. 'Nothing too dressy. Plenty of people will go in jeans. After all, it's only dancing in the square.'

'Oh,' her face fell. She fancied something more feminine than jeans.

'But a pretty skirt and top would do fine.'

'Great, I've got a couple with me. Thanks, Anne.'

Going quickly up the stairs to her room she decided she would type up her notes from this morning's interview with Anne and would also include something about the windmill which would be a nice bit of local colour.

Hopefully she could have it all done

by dinner time and then she could relax this evening and make an early start tomorrow.

Perhaps after dinner she could concentrate on deciding what to wear for the dance. If she could get ahead with her work she could leave herself plenty of time to spend on her appearance.

For who knew what the evening would bring?

5

Next day she decided to stay inside the chateau and continue working her way through the rooms. She took pictures and wrote descriptions of each one.

No two rooms were alike either in size or aspect, but all were beautiful with old French beds and wardrobes. Most had recent ensuite showers fitted in ways which blended in unobtrusively.

Each was also unique largely due to the way the main building was designed so every one was individual and charming.

At the start of the job she felt like an intruder as she took her position in a room and drew in the atmosphere so that she could write an informative and enticing report. But now she was used to roaming around with her notebook and camera, although she always checked with Anne where she would be working.

In the middle of the afternoon she ran up to her room, humming a tune and feeling happy to be there. She flung herself on the bed and stretched luxuriously.

Everything was going well with her work — the people were an added bonus and her relationship with both Anne and Robert was a friendly one. Her walk yesterday with Pierre had also been taken on the most friendly of terms.

Indeed she had the strong impression that Pierre would like to be more than friends. Annick — she pushed the girl from her mind for it was better not to think about her.

Then of course there was Gerrard. If she didn't take herself in hand, she knew she could easily fall in love with him.

For a few more minutes she indulged herself by thinking about the chateau and its occupants. Then with a sudden burst of energy that had its roots in happiness, she sprang up and reached for her laptop. There was, as usual, the day's notes to be typed and a work plan formed for the next day.

Later, after a shower and with freshly-washed hair, she made up her face lightly. Next she slipped a black cotton skirt over her head and teamed it with a halter-necked black cotton top.

Hannah was not a vain girl, but she couldn't stop a smile of pure pleasure when she looked at herself in the mirror. Her hair was shining and fair and her dark eyes glowed. The walk in the sun yesterday had added a flush to her skin and the dark clothes contrasted with her fairness.

The other three were waiting in the hall as she came down the stairs. What an entrance. She should be sweeping down in a ball gown and she nearly giggled and hoped she wouldn't trip and spoil the effect.

'Ah, there you are.' Gerrard was the first to speak and he reached out a hand to assist her down the last couple of stairs. In his eyes she could see admiration and she felt wonderfully feminine as she joined the group.

''Allo.' Annick's smile was tight, but she looked dainty and elfin in off-white. Then with her eyes on Hannah, she slowly and deliberately took Gerrard's arm. 'Come,' she said, 'we must go.' She led the way out to the car where she made sure she was in the passenger seat.

'You look very lovely,' said Pierre and she had no alternative but to walk beside him down the steps. Determined not to let the French girl spoil her evening, Hannah settled in the back of the car beside Pierre.

★   ★   ★

As they reached the village, Hannah couldn't resist a gasp of surprise. The place was transformed. A lorry was parked sideways at one corner of the square. The side was dropped down so that the base of the vehicle formed a stage and on it appeared to be a complete music unit with lights and microphone.

Gerrard laughed at her bewildered face. 'It's entirely self-contained, even to its own generator. It will make a tour of neighbouring villages during the summer.'

'It's utterly fantastic.' She couldn't drag her gaze away. 'It all looks so professional.' Gerrard turned her towards him and, smiling with shy pleasure, she met such warmth in his eyes that she felt herself flush.

Then from the corner of her eye, she saw the long painted nails of Annick touch Gerrard's sleeve as she asked him to dance. There was a momentary hesitation before he took her hand and escorted her on to the floor.

Noting with satisfaction the loud music with a very pronounced beat, which meant they would be dancing apart, she watched as they positioned themselves and her heart plummeted as she saw Annick use her body to full advantage.

'Come on.' She started at Pierre's voice. 'We can't let them get all the attention.' He caught her hand and pulled her on to the floor.

Normally reluctant to let herself go completely, she was at once relaxed with Pierre. He wasn't a brilliant dancer but his enthusiasm was infectious and she was soon taking his lead in a display which normally she would be reluctant to follow. Perhaps, her mind told her, the French air has something to do with it. She twirled around with arms high above her head and suddenly she was very near to Gerrard and their eyes met.

From that moment she kept her eyes firmly on her own partner, smiling happily at him and didn't notice the way Gerrard watched her or the expression on his face.

Sitting out the next couple of dances at a café table, they chatted and the men didn't appear to notice that she and Annick spoke very little to each other. Once more she took the floor with Pierre, a slower number this time and wondered if Gerrard would ask her to dance. Surely good manners alone required they change partners.

Returning to the table, she began to feel distinctly on edge and lost interest in the conversation going on around her. Once or twice she tried speaking to Annick, making a supreme effort to be friendly, but her overtures were quickly rebuffed in a way only another woman could understand.

Staring at her glass, she wondered how she could possibly long for and yet dread the idea of dancing with him. The evening was wearing on and the music becoming moody and romantic. If he asked her now, there would be no dancing apart, each doing their own steps. Indeed, she could already see couples with their arms entwined and cheeks together.

Biting her lip, she knew she was terrified of being held closely in his arms. If she found herself in that position, she knew she'd end up fighting for control. In fact, fighting against an unknown weakness in herself.

'Hannah.' He was standing beside her and she had no alternative but to take the hand he was offering and get to her feet. Reluctantly, she allowed him to guide her on to the centre of the square where it was warm and unbelievably crowded and nowhere she could run to escape. Shaking her head, she couldn't cope with her thoughts. Why should she want to escape, it was only a dance.

For a moment they stared at one another and the expression in his eyes warned her not to try to leave him. Hemmed in by bodies, the music throbbed in her head as everything she feared started to take place. She was terribly afraid, but when she tried to find the cause of her terror, it was still only the fear of being in his arms.

Just one dance she promised herself,

surely she could cope with just one dance. An arm came around her back and holding herself stiffly, she tried to put as much air between them as possible. But in such a crowded space, it was a hopeless task.

Trying to keep her distance while following his lead would have been funny if it hadn't been so awful and she suppressed a wild panicky need to giggle.

Risking a glance from under her lashes, she received the full force of blue eyes that appeared to be searching her soul. He raised one eyebrow as though inquiring why she was behaving in such a way and then as though at the end of his patience, he grasped her tightly, wrapping his arms around her so she could barely move.

They were so closely entwined that she could feel every movement of his body. When his right leg glided forward, her left leg slid back as though their limbs were joined. She could not stop moving even if she wanted to and now she was no longer sure exactly what she did want.

As they drifted around, she turned at his command, completely under his control. She was his puppet. He only had to pull the strings and she moved at his bidding.

There was something delightfully irresponsible about not being answerable for her own actions. It wasn't her fault they were dancing so closely. Whoever was watching, it really didn't matter and she stopped worrying, knowing that everything was beyond her control.

'Put your arms around my neck,' he whispered into her hair.

So she just had to wind her arms around him, her fingers of their own accord lightly caressing his nape. It wasn't her decision, only something she had to do. Never had she felt so deliciously relaxed, so delicately sensuous. Lifting her arms, she allowed her fingers to creep up into his hair and the movement brought her even closer to him.

'Hmm . . . ' she sighed softly and then became aware of some announcement that was being relayed.

'What did he say?' she asked as the sound was so distorted she couldn't make out a word.

'He said it is a very special dance.'

'What kind of special?' She laughed up at him.

'We'll have to see, won't we?' And he wrapped his arms even tighter around her.

Then the lights dimmed and she gave into the urge to lean into him and put her head on his shoulder.

She hadn't noticed that the evening shadows had gathered and without the bright lights, the square was quite dark.

Dipping his head lower, his lips brushed her eyelids.

Then the lights dimmed again.

Closing her eyes, she drifted into another world, an unknown, but exciting world, where the only things that mattered were feelings and touching against the background of the haunting melody.

It was perfect and then the lights dimmed further as the music changed to an even slower tempo.

His lips were against her hair and she could feel their softness lightly over her head and forehead and knew soon they would be lingering over her mouth. It was inevitable. She had fought this feeling the past few days but no longer, because now she was impatient for his touch.

He spoke as though tuned into her thoughts. 'Do you know how much I want to kiss you?'

Lifting stargazed eyes to his face, she smiled seductively and nodded. The crowded room faded and desperate for the touch of his lips against her, she clutched at his neck, trying to bring his head down lower.

As they swayed round, grasping each other, she knew that when the music stopped her world would crumble and she would sink down as though her life was over. He found her lips in a long kiss, then gasping, she looked wildly around, but no-one was looking at them. In fact, it was difficult to see the other couples.

Why don't we leave, she silently asked him, trying to get the message across with her eyes. But now her head was tucked almost under his chin and it was impossible.

They could leave now while the lights were low and no-one could see them. Her head spun as faintly she thought of Pierre and Annick and knew they wouldn't be able to leave them behind.

Swallowing convulsively, she tried to push away the longing for them to be completely alone, but it was like pushing against cotton wool and refused to go away.

Like a shower of cold water, the music stopped and the lights flicked up. Blinking rapidly, she wondered where the light and people had come from and where was the Gerrard who held her so closely? He had gone and in his place was a man who pulled her lightly from him and was able to smile at the other couples on the floor.

Closing her eyes, she tried to burrow nearer to him, wanting to get back into her warm world of love. But like a dream that drifts away upon waking, it disappeared. Something beautiful and elusive was within her grasp and as her hand reached to clasp it, a cruel wind blew it beyond her reach.

Making their way back to the table, she was glad of the arm thrown around so casually but almost supporting her. As she sank on to her seat, the firm warm arm withdrew and it was almost like saying goodbye.

It was obvious when they returned that the other couple had been sitting out during the dancing and Annick looked at her sharply.

The rest of the evening faded into obscurity as she spoke when spoken to, managed to smile and sip more wine. In fact, all things considered, she was developing quite a liking for the drink.

Gerrard behaved normally. So normally

that she thought she must have imagined his caresses until he looked straight at her and she saw the expression in his eyes. Embarrassingly and before she could control it, a flush spread over her face and neck and shakily picking up her half full glass, she swallowed the contents in a gulp.

She couldn't remember ever drinking so much before, but it in no way dimmed the ache inside her but rather accentuated her feelings. These feelings were fast gathering into a cloud, a softly floating mass that was slowly swelling inside her and waiting for something to happen.

Hopelessly trying to be bright and normal, she sank back in her chair and gave up. Maybe the others would think she was tired, but it didn't matter what they thought as long as it wasn't the truth.

She danced again with Pierre, but everything that followed was an anti-climax. The whole focus of the evening had been when the lights were dim, the music sweet and Gerrard's arms were about her.

Now and again she glanced at her watch, wondering what time they would leave or more to the point, how they would leave. Gerrard was now behaving so casually that the awful thought occurred that perhaps their dance had meant nothing to him.

Pierre quickly claimed her for the last dance and feeling guilty, she tried to sparkle as she remembered he was really her escort for the evening. 'Must do this again,' he murmured into her hair.

'Yes.' It took all her willpower not to pull away, knowing that after Gerrard she couldn't bear anyone else to be so close.

Eventually they bundled into the car and once again Annick was in the front. Pierre took her hand and moved nearer and it took all her willpower to leave her hand in his.

If she pushed him away, it would be obvious to the front passengers that something was going on in the back. She didn't want to give anyone that impression, especially Gerrard.

Even when they reached the chateau, there was no opportunity for her and Gerrard to be alone, but she took comfort in his glance and the warm squeeze of his hand as he bade her goodnight. Lightly he kissed her on both cheeks, knowing that the other pair were watching.

'Goodnight, Hannah,' he said quite loudly, and then whispered, 'until tomorrow.'

She floated up the wide, elegant staircase like a heroine of old and once in her room it was a long time before she managed to get into bed. With her mind full of lovely dreams, she sat on the window seat, looking into the darkened grounds and thought about Gerrard.

6

Until tomorrow,' he had said and she hugged the words to herself all night long. They were still on her lips when she awoke the next morning. In fact, she wondered for a moment if she had actually uttered them through the night. Well at least, she thought, the walls of the chateau are thick and no-one could hear my silly mumblings.

As she lay warm and content in the large bed, she knew that whatever the weather it was going to be a wonderful day. For come rain or shine Gerrard would surely tell her what his feelings were towards her.

For a moment, doubt crept into her heart as she asked herself, just what were his feelings towards her. There was also the possibility that he didn't have any feelings towards her at all, but the way he'd held her during the dance last night must have meant something.

But of course, there was competition for there was always Annick and she was most definitely interested in Gerrard and deeply resentful of any attention he paid to any other girl.

But surely if he wanted Annick, he would have done something about it before this. No, she was sure the feelings were all on the side of Annick. Before allowing any more doubts to come to mind she sprang from the bed, ran to the window and pulled back the curtains.

Just as she knew it would be, the sun was coming up and shining through a slight mist. Then something caught her eye and looking down she saw Gerrard standing beneath her window and waving for her to come down.

She could hardly believe her eyes when she saw him there and then she held up both hands to tell him she'd be down in ten minutes. Quickly she dressed in shirt, sandals and jeans, and as she swiftly pulled on her clothes she thought how ridiculous that in a building this size, there never seemed to be anywhere for them to be on their own.

Each time they'd returned from an evening out, there had been others calling out to them and Gerrard had stayed behind to join the social gathering.

Creeping down the stairs, she caught a glimpse of the hall clock. It was so early and she looked again, surprised that it was only six a.m. What on earth was he doing outside her window at this hour?

As she scuttled quickly through to the back entrance she could hear Marie shuffling around and was careful not to be seen. There was no way she could cope with questions as to what she was doing at this hour of the morning.

'Gerrard,' she breathed, 'what are you doing here so early?'

'Hannah,' his voice was low and he said her name slowly as though it was an endearment.

He was going to kiss her, she was certain, but he turned away and then taking her hand, he led her swiftly round to the side of the chateau where he stopped and took her into his arms.

'We're alone at last,' he whispered. 'I couldn't sleep and went for a walk and then I stood beneath your window and just hoped that if I thought of you hard enough, you would know I was there.'

'Of course I was thinking of you, but I didn't know you were down here.' She nestled closer. 'I didn't know you were such a romantic. Do you know we're acting just like Romeo and Juliet?' She giggled. 'Although we're a little old to be doing balcony scenes.'

'Where's your romance,' he hugged her tightly. 'No-one is ever too young or too old, especially in France.'

Then she felt she was melting as his mouth found her own. His lips were soft but firm and his kiss was what she'd been waiting for ever since she arrived, for now she was ready to admit that she had fallen completely in love with Gerrard. Dissolving in a world of her own feelings she almost missed what he was saying.

'Tonight, after dinner, we'll slip away and go down to the village for a drink or coffee so that we are on our own and we can talk.'

'Have we got things to say?' She leaned back and looked provocatively up at him.

'After the dance last night I know I have and I hoped perhaps that you wanted to hear them.' He looked down at her and his eyes were full of an expression which looked very close to love. 'Hannah, I . . .'

'Yes,' she gasped eagerly.

'Hannah, I . . .' He shook his head slightly. 'No, it's not the right place here because any moment someone is going to see us. Claude will be about soon.'

'Yes, Marie is already pottering around the kitchen.'

'It will wait though, Hannah. It will wait until tonight.'

'By the way,' he said as they walked

back, 'have you noticed anything suspicious about Robert?'

'Robert,' she repeated vaguely, and then remembered he wanted her to report on the older man and the precious moment was spoiled. 'I've been too busy to even look at the tapestry myself during the last couple of days and he spends most of his time with Anne.'

'Yes, Mother and Robert. What do you make of them, Hannah? You've got a fresh eye as you're new here. How do they seem to you?'

Feeling disappointed that their moment was already over, she had difficulty keeping her temper.

'Like good friends,' she snapped. She was far more interested in her own romance with him than that of his mother.

Gerrard had certainly not tuned into her mood and muttered, 'I worry for her. I think she's very vulnerable.'

Of course, she then felt totally selfish because he was obviously concerned for her and had a perfect right to be.

'I must get changed and plan my day,' she said abruptly as they reached the hall.

'I've a lot on as well,' he said as she turned away from him, 'but I'll see you at dinner or before.'

★ ★ ★

Once in her room, she began to get her things together almost on automatic pilot while her mind started a debate, asking her if it was just possible he only appeared interested in her so that she could report on Robert. Maybe he wasn't interested in her romantically at all.

Later, as she made her way to the kitchen, where the family took breakfast at one end of the large tiled room, she noticed a strange atmosphere.

Gerrard was missing, well that wasn't unusual, but Anne and Robert had their heads together and Anne's fingers were strumming on the table.

'I shall have to be here today now, Robert, you must understand that I can't be out when he comes. We will have to change our arrangements.'

Marie stood a large pot of coffee on the table and as no-one appeared inclined to include her in much conversation, Hannah ate a roll and croissant and quickly left the room wondering who it was who was coming and ruining Anne and Robert's arrangement for the day.

Two hours later with her morning work going well, she decided to give herself a well-earned coffee break. She was surprised she had been able to concentrate on work at all when her mind was full of Gerrard.

Halfway down the stairs, she stopped as there was the sound of a car pulling up. As she came slowly down the rest of the stairs, Anne suddenly appeared below her and opened the large front door and made her way down the outside steps.

Then there was a slam of a car door

and the sound of feet that ran lightly up the steps as a small boy rushed from the car and into the arms of Anne.

'Grandmere!' he shrieked, 'Grandmere!'

Hannah stood perfectly immobilised. The child had called out Grandmere. Who could possibly be the parents?

Surely Gerrard had said he was an only child, but he must have a brother or sister. But no, Anne had once mentioned that Gerrard was all she had.

Transfixed she watched as the child saw someone over Anne's shoulder and started to wriggle down from Anne and rushed up to a man who now stood at the open door.

'Jean,' the man exclaimed with pleasure and picked up the child and held him high in his arms. The man was Gerrard.

Suddenly she felt sick and the blood left her face. In all their conversations together there appeared to be one important point he hadn't thought to mention. The fact that he was married, and not only that, but married with a child.

How had she misread the signs and missed something that should have been obvious? But there were no photographs around of Gerrard with a wife and child and no-one had even mentioned the name of his wife.

Slowly she turned away but she moved slowly as in a dream. Something new and wonderful had started to blossom inside her. Something that was essential between her and this man. But it had no substance and was just a tune on the breeze which was blown away and soon forgotten.

All thoughts of coffee fled from her mind, in fact she doubted that her stomach could cope with anything, she was in such a turmoil. Slowly and with her shoulders slumped, she turned away from the scene beneath her. No-one had noticed she was there and she managed to drag herself back up to her room.

So much for her career girl image, she thought, I'm just like any other vulnerable girl, put me beside an interesting man and I fall at his feet and wait for him to step on me.

For a moment she felt like pulling out of the job. But even as the idea was conceived, it was abandoned because she couldn't let the agency down.

In any case, what could she tell them? She certainly couldn't risk giving the impression she couldn't handle the work. Definitely the truth was something she must keep to herself. She just could not be so unprofessional as to allow personalities to get in the way of the job.

This was supposed to be her big break and she'd let herself become involved so very easily. She began to pace the room and then stopped herself. What on earth was she doing acting like this?

The best thing she could do today was to keep out of everyone's way. Fortunately there was a chocolate bar in her bag and that would have to do for lunch.

After typing her notes from the morning she knew she'd never concentrate on work for the rest of the day, and on an impulse left her room and wandered up to the gallery to see the tapestry.

Robert was there with his reference book. 'Just the lady I need to help me,' he said as she stood beside him. 'Too much going on downstairs for me today so I've escaped up here.'

She was desperate to ask him what the situation was down there but bit back the words and peered at the page he held open.

'Look, I'm sure this is it. The date, design, colour, they're all there, just the signature is impossible for me to make out.'

'I think it's faded in that corner, but I'm sure you're right in identifying it and if you're right it's worth a whole heap of money.' She continued slowly, 'but at least it's French. I did wonder if it was Belgian at first, but it is certainly very valuable.'

'You're right, my dear. I must have a word with Anne. She doesn't take the value of the items here seriously enough. It worries me that there will be a burglary and I keep warning her but she doesn't take any notice.'

She nodded. 'I agree, Anne hasn't got the interest.' She turned to look up at him, 'But I thought that was because of you, Robert?'

His eyes twinkled, 'I live in hope, but you know I can't stay here for ever. I'll have to return to my gallery soon.'

'I suppose you'd like to take the tapestry with you,' she said impulsively and suddenly knew that his answer would tell her what she needed to know.

He smiled, that typical American smile, wide and sincere with a flash of white teeth. 'I admit it would look good on my wall, but it would never be for sale and it would only go back with me if Anne came with it.' He smiled again.

'But I expect you've guessed all this.'

She nodded, warming once more to this friendly American and touched his arm gently. 'I hope it works out for you,' she said softly and left him with his book.

If there was one thing she was certain about, it was that Robert was not a prospective thief. He was far too open and sincere.

Well, she could put Gerrard's mind at rest about Robert at last. Then she remembered the child who'd arrived and was more than ever convinced that he was only interested in her so that she could report to him.

She needed to get out of the building and into the fresh air so she moved quietly, gliding like a ghost and keeping away from any part of the building where she could hear voices until, for the second time that day, she was outside. But this time there was no Gerrard looking as though he loved her.

Well, one thing, she wouldn't be going out with him this evening. In fact, the way she felt, she never wanted to see or speak to him again.

Walking briskly along the drive, she met Pierre who suddenly appeared from the side of the chateau.

'Where are you going?' he called to her.

'Just a walk, I think better when I walk.' She managed a laugh.

'I'll come along with you for a while if you don't mind. I need to call on someone who lives nearby.'

He made no comment about the goings-on at the chateau so perhaps, she wondered, he hadn't called there yet. He'd obviously changed his mind when he saw her. They were friendly, but there was no reason for him to put himself out to walk with her. She frowned and wondered what was in his mind.

They walked swiftly but in silence for a while, and then Pierre said, over-casually, 'What do you think of the tapestry in the gallery?'

'Oh.' For a moment she forgot her

own troubles. 'It's just wonderful. Robert and I are always discussing it. In fact,' she joked, 'we meet quite frequently in front of it.' Then she thought that maybe she'd said too much. He knew Robert was interested in art and by mentioning his name she had given extra importance to the tapestry. Then she shrugged her shoulders, it really couldn't matter.

'Valuable, would you say?'

'Oh, very, I should think.' Then she stopped for there was something in his voice as he asked the question. A certain edge that showed more than casual interest and once again she could have bitten her tongue.

'Do you think Robert would like to take it back to the States? I know he has an interest in art.'

'What a strange question,' she turned to look at him, trying to make out his expression.

'But, if it is valuable, he may be interested. Have you discussed it with him?'

She felt her temper rise. It was not his place to question her about anything, especially the valuables in the chateau.

Mentally, she counted to ten and then said quite levelly, 'Not in that context, no. Besides, it's none of my business, but I do know that it's not always easy to ship art to another country.'

'Gerrard would like things to stay as they are and I agree with him, for I believe valuable objects like that should stay where they belong, in France.'

Hannah was surprised at the vehemence in his voice.

'You're quite a French revolutionist.' She laughed uneasily trying to lighten the atmosphere. She didn't like where the conversation was going and hoped they could change the subject.

He must have picked up on her thoughts for after a few minutes, he seemed to change back into the pleasant companion he'd been the day when they walked together to the windmill.

Soon afterwards, he took a small turning and they parted. Hannah was relieved to see him go, for this was a different Pierre and although she'd not had a lot to do with him since she arrived, he'd always been pleasant and charming.

She'd genuinely liked Pierre. The whole thing was ridiculous, first Gerrard, now Pierre. What was the problem with the men concerned with this job? Only Robert appeared completely genuine and he was the one whom Gerrard distrusted.

Anyway, it wasn't her problem. The quandary that confronted her today was how to make herself scarce. It was ridiculous as there were so few people here but they were all disturbing in their way.

Whenever Gerrard and her wanted to be alone, especially when they returned from the village dance, the place had seemed full of people and there was no privacy at all. They appeared a normal friendly family, but that family had its secrets and each member had some kind of mystery.

Was the tapestry in any danger? She couldn't believe that it was, the whole idea was ridiculous. It was developing into a mystery. Why did Gerrard suspect Robert, and now Pierre was behaving strangely with his questions.

If she could just get through the next few hours and have a good night's sleep, then perhaps tomorrow she could cope with what was happening at the chateau.

7

Her immediate problem was getting through the rest of the day and she slowed her steps to give herself time to think. Somehow she must keep out of everyone's way, particularly Gerrard, until she felt more in control of the situation.

Whatever happened, there was no possible way she could sit round the table this evening at dinner, knowing that Gerrard was not only married, but had a child. How could she face him? She must have time to get used to the idea, if, of course, she ever did.

It was his tenderness from this morning that hurt her the most and it was something she would never forget. She had been completely taken in by him because he'd given the impression of being totally sincere and she had believed him.

Years ago, he would have been called a cad, she grumbled to herself and there were all sorts of names she could happily call him now to give vent to her feelings. Her mouth was dry and she felt vague sensations of shock at his treachery, or was that too strong a word for it?

Anyway, dinner was definitely out. She was sure the food would choke her as she remembered his kiss and the way it made her feel. Stupid, stupid woman, she told herself. Why did you allow yourself to be involved, but it had happened without her realising it and now she had to go on with her job. She just hoped she could find the strength of mind to get through it.

As she reached the chateau, she bypassed the main entrance and skirted round the side where she found a stone bench and sank on to it gratefully. It was quiet and peaceful and she would have liked to put her head back and drift into happier thoughts.

She couldn't sit here for the rest of

the day so just what was she going to do. She could always stay in her room, but she would have to make excuses not to go down to dinner which could be tricky.

Her head slumped and then trying to sit up straighter she looked straight ahead and directly in front of her were the garages. Surely somehow she could make her escape but what to do. She couldn't help herself to one of the cars.

Then her mood lifted as inspiration came suddenly into her mind. There was a way she could escape. It would be discreet and quiet and springing up she walked across where, as luck would have it, she found Claude.

'Bonjour, Claude,' she started and then broke into English. 'I need to go to the village and wondered if you would get Madame's bike out for me again.' She smiled at him knowing that she hadn't actually asked Anne, but she would deal with that problem later.

'Of course, Mademoiselle 'annah, but

would you prefer that I take you in the car?'

That was the last thing she wanted. Panic took over and she could hardly stop herself from stepping back or running away. But she managed to stand still and then hanging on to her pride said, 'Oh thank you, but no. I shall enjoy the ride again.'

He nodded at her and went to the back of one of the garages and came out pushing the bike. 'There you are. You know the way,' he said and dusted off the saddle with such a flourish that she felt quite tearful. Here, at least, was someone who cared about her welfare.

Taking the handlebars, she wheeled the bike away and called over her shoulder, 'Please tell Marie that I won't be at dinner tonight.' Then before he could question her remark she swung on to the saddle and pedalled like crazy along the drive. Not wanting anyone in the house to see her she only slowed down when she was safely on the road leading to the village.

As she rode, the exercise appeared to be good therapy for her spirits began to rise. The situation was her own fault for she had forgotten why she was here and had begun to treat it as part work and part holiday.

Put me near an attractive man and I go all foolish and imagine myself falling in love. But she had the strangest feeling that she really had fallen in love with Gerrard.

Losing her concentration, she started to wobble and an oncoming motorist glared at her and shook his fist as she veered to the wrong side of the road. She gritted her teeth and resolutely pushed thoughts of romance firmly away and concentrated on what she would do when she reached the village.

As it happened, she automatically stopped at the café, and propping up the bike outside, she took a seat and picked up the menu. After all she'd cancelled dinner at the chateau so there was no reason why she should starve just because she didn't want to join the family tonight.

'A glass of wine mademoiselle?' The young waiter stopped at her table.

She nodded, 'White please. The house wine will be fine.'

'You take dinner?' he questioned again.

She studied the menu again. Why not? Why not treat herself to something nice to eat. She chose a tomato salad followed by a plate of cooked meats with a baguette.

As her simple meal progressed, her confidence rose. Just one thing worried her and it was that she hadn't asked permission from Anne to borrow the bike but she'd apologise tomorrow.

Later, while sipping her coffee she noticed Pierre and another young man walking towards the café. Oh dear, they would be sure to join her and that wasn't what she wanted.

However, Pierre looked surprised to see her and after a brief greeting, turned away. He said something in French to the other man and when she heard the reply, she recognised the voice.

He was the man Pierre had been speaking to near her window the night she'd arrived. Now why had Pierre avoided her because it was pretty obvious that was why he had turned away.

'Mademoiselle?' The waiter was at her side again, 'you would like more coffee?' He was smiling and obviously eager to practise his English.

She decided to see if she could find out more about Pierre and his companion. 'No thank you,' she replied and then looked up at him, returning his smile. 'Those two men who came in and then quickly went out, did you see one of them speak to me?'

'Ah yes, he comes here frequently, he is Pierre . . . '

'And the other one?' she interrupted.

His smile disappeared. 'The other man, Mademoiselle, does not belong to the village, but has been here a few times recently.' He leaned towards her,

'I hear things about him that I do not like.'

She became alert and sat up straighter. 'What kind of things?'

'He is what you English call 'shabby'.'

'Shabby?'

He looked thoughtful and then his face brightened. 'No, no, not shabby.' He thought for a moment. 'He is someone who does not always say the truth. Someone a little suspicious.' And then he beamed. 'Shady, M'amselle, that is the word I am seeking.'

She let the word sink in while she congratulated him on his excellent English and felt duty bound to have another cup of coffee.

*　　*　　*

To get rid of some time, she pushed the bike around the village, but there was nothing to merit staying there any longer and reluctantly she turned back the way she had come.

On the way back, she pedalled slowly

and thought about Pierre and the other man. The Pierre who was with her today had shown a totally different side to him. For a while he had not been the polite and attentive Frenchman she'd first met and now he was presumably in the company of someone 'shady.'

But there was nothing sinister about Pierre. He appeared very straightforward and was in line for the job of running the hotel. Their last conversation flashed into her mind for there had been something strange and contrived about the questions which he asked.

There was something odd, now she thought about it, and for a moment her mind jumped to conclusions and took a terrifying leap as she wondered about his interest in the tapestry. She tried not to think about anything after that for her thoughts were becoming far too jumbled.

Her luck was certainly in, for again there was no-one around when she eventually returned to the house. For a moment she hesitated, wondering what to do with the bike. She couldn't afford to draw attention to herself and then, making up her mind, she dismounted and quickly wheeled it round to the main garage and propped it against the wall.

Ignoring the imposing front entrance, she found that the back door of the kitchen area was unlocked and crept through the house feeling like a criminal. She told herself that it was ridiculous and she should just stride through and make as much noise as she liked, but she knew she couldn't deal with the situation tonight. Maybe tomorrow when she'd had time to become used to it.

As she gazed around, there was no sign of anything that could belong to a child, and for a mad moment she thought she might have imagined it all. Then there were voices behind the closed door of the sitting-room and she quickened her steps and managed to gain the staircase without being seen.

As she placed one foot on the bottom

of the wide staircase she was conscious of the thudding of her heart and realised how tense she'd been. But now she was almost safe and trying to relax her shoulders she made her way up the stairs.

Trying to be quick and quiet at the same time was not easy in an old property where everything tended to creak.

Reaching the top had never been so long, but nobody seemed to be aware of her return and at last she reached her bedroom door.

The bed had never looked so inviting and she decided to undress swiftly and lay on its comforting softness. She made her way towards it, shaking off one shoe as she went and then with her foot lifted to rid herself of the other one, she knew she was not alone. Her head snapped up and she saw him.

In the room where shadows of night were already falling, he rose from where he was sitting in the chair at the window and stood straight and stiff.

She swallowed back a scream as she recognised him.

He didn't speak, but just looked at her. She was left feeling a fool with one shoe off and one on and suddenly she had to confront him and hopped across towards the window. Her whole body was full of mixed emotions, puzzlement, hurt and foremost of all, fury.

'What on earth are you doing skulking in my room?' In spite of herself her voice rose shrilly and her hands clenched at her sides.

'I'm waiting for you, my dear Hannah,' he said slowly with an edge of sarcasm. 'We had an arrangement, remember? We were going to meet after dinner.'

'Yes, well . . . '

'But you didn't even come to dinner, and Claude said you'd gone to the village. So who did you meet, was it Pierre? I knew you'd been with him earlier.'

The blood flooded her face and she could hardly get the words out. 'What do you mean, I'd been with him? You appear to have been spying on me all day, and frankly I'm surprised you had the time.' The words were said through gritted teeth.

They glared at each other, both standing their ground like two animals who would eventually close in for the kill, although from time to time she tottered and was in danger of overbalancing.

'Why are you so friendly with Pierre?'

She nearly choked at his presumption. How dare he say that when she had discovered he had been stringing her along. 'Why didn't you tell me you were married?' Suddenly her voice cut off in a sob. 'After this morning why didn't you tell me?'

'Married?'

He was a wonderful actor because his surprise appeared to be genuine.

'Yes, married and a father,' she almost sobbed and had a job to hang on to her pride. Then feeling at such a disadvantage standing on one foot, she kicked the other shoe across the room. At least now she could face him standing firm and square.

'Father?'

She could have sworn he was genuinely puzzled.

'What are you talking about. I'm certainly not married and to my knowledge I am not a father.'

He came towards her and she panicked and stepped back. She backed away from him for several steps until something told her that she had nearly reached the bed.

Not wanting the indignity of toppling backwards across it, she at last stood still and trembled slightly as she wondered what he would do. But he gently but firmly held the top of her arms. 'Now start at the beginning and tell me what has happened.'

Their gazes locked and she saw that his eyes were tender like they'd been earlier in the day. But, she hardened her heart for there was no getting away from it and he couldn't talk his way out of this. She tried to step back but his hands held her firm.

Then the words came rushing out, 'It was this morning. I heard a car and then a child came running up the steps calling, Grandmere,' she hesitated. 'Your mother picked him up.'

She stopped as her mouth suddenly dried and licked her lips. 'Then the child saw you and rushed to you and you scooped him up. I was in the hall,' she admitted, 'and you didn't see me and then I crept away.'

He raised one eyebrow, 'And that was enough to damn me in your eyes?'

'Yes,' she looked him straight in the eyes and held herself rigid. 'It was enough, it was more than enough.'

8

His eyes looked so honest and true that she couldn't speak. What had happened to her doubts, for they were fast leaving her mind. Her head started to spin and she squeezed her eyes tightly shut. Surely she couldn't be wrong, it wasn't possible.

Perhaps the day had been some awful nightmare and now she had woken. Stifling a nervous giggle she thought about pinching herself to see if she really was awake.

At last she managed to wriggle away from him and went to stand at the window, taking care to keep some space around herself. A breeze blew through the open window and ruffled his hair.

He looked so perfect that he could have been posing for a photograph. He was too big, too real and she knew that she would have problems resisting him.

At this moment, she didn't want him near her, she wanted her own space around her so that she needn't look at him and doubt her sanity.

He let her stand alone and for a moment a coolness spread through her as she thought he would leave the room and knew she wanted him to stay.

But impossibly, it seemed he could read her mind. 'I know you don't want me near you, but I'm not leaving until this is straightened out between us. I'll stay in this room all night if necessary.'

She lifted her arms and hugged herself, hoping he would take the hint and keep his distance. She couldn't cope when he was near her and there had been too much happening during this one day. Too many emotions to deal with and in the end it was all so tiring that she felt exhausted.

He stared at her and repeated, 'So you damn me? Hannah, I thought you felt the same way I feel about you.'

Swinging round, she faced him. 'I do, well I did but you lied to me. How could you do that, how could you lie to me?' She stopped abruptly, 'This morning I thought, I thought . . . ' How could she admit that she'd imagined that he said, 'je t'aime.' The words, I love you, were wonderful in English, but when he murmured them in French, it was the most romantic thing any one had ever said to her.

A muscle moved in his face and she heard the hardness when he spoke. 'I would never lie to you, never. How could you think I would not tell you the truth always.'

She drew in a jerky breath and the words she wanted to say wouldn't come. She just stood dumbly watching him and then she started to shiver.

'Let's sit down,' he said calmly. 'Are you cold? Shall I close the window?'

'No, no,' she answered quickly knowing she needed the fresh air to stop herself from falling under his spell. Then she looked vaguely around the room. There was just one armchair and the bed.

In a couple of strides he was across the room and taking her hand. 'I won't bite you know. I won't even sit too close to you.' He smiled and led her to the bed.

Her body allowed him to lead her from the window. Her mind had lost control and she went with him, like a child. Suddenly she was glad to sit down. Too much emotions had taken the strength from her legs.

He cleared his throat and she sat waiting and wondering if she could believe what he was going to say.

He made a great production of not sitting too near to her, but reached across for her hand, held it and started to stroke her fingers.

'The boy's name is Jean and he is not my son.'

She turned her face swiftly towards him trying to read the expression in those deep blue eyes, as she gasped, 'But . . . but . . .'

He put a finger over her lips. 'Please Hannah, let me finish. As I say he is not my son, although in some ways I wish he were for he is the most delightful child, full of enthusiasm for life.'

'But he called your mother, Grandmere.' Angrily she twisted her head, throwing off his finger from her mouth and snatched her hand away. He was lying again, he must be, there was no other explanation. 'Do you take me for a fool?' she said coldly. 'You told me you were an only child, like me, we discussed it soon after I arrived. So he must be your child.'

It was all too much and she covered her face with her hands in an effort to hold back tears. 'You come to my room and invade my space just when I want to be alone, and for what?' Her voice rose and she hated the shrill sound she could hear. 'To lie to me.' She shrugged away the arm that reached out for her.

For a moment there was silence and then Gerrard cleared his throat and looked down at the floor. She could sense that he was uneasy and thought it was because he felt guilty. When he began to speak his voice was low.

'He is not my son, he is my nephew.'

'Nephew,' she interrupted, 'but how can he be?'

'Please Hannah, let me finish. I don't think I actually said I was an only child, probably said something like, 'there's only me.' It's what I say when I don't or can't feel I can fully explain about our family.'

His usually deep voice became soft and she had difficulty hearing some of the words and she leaned towards him.

'I had a sister, a little older than me and we were very close.' He stopped as though it was difficult for him to continue. 'She married and had a son but,' his voice quickened and the words came out in a rush. 'At the end the marriage wasn't happy and eventually there was another man.'

Her head began to thud, what was happening? Had she really misjudged him because if that was so, she had hurt him terribly by bringing all his grief about his sister to the surface and misunderstanding him so badly.

'I'm so terribly sorry. I . . . ' She stuttered as her mouth felt as though it had stopped working. 'Please don't tell me anymore, it must be so painful for you.'

He went on as though she hadn't spoken. 'The other man was very successful and my sister was flattered. One day they were together in a light aircraft which he owned. They were going to visit friends, but the plane crashed. We never knew how or why only that my sister had gone for ever.'

She reached for his hand. 'I'm so sorry,' she said quietly. 'I know that saying sorry is so inadequate, but I'm sorry not only for what happened but also for the way I've behaved. I should have trusted you . . . '

'Don't worry, cherie. Shall I tell you the rest of the story.'

She squeezed his fingers, trying to comfort him in some way. 'No don't Gerrard. It's obviously difficult for you to talk about it and you shouldn't have

131

to relive it all just to explain it to me.'

'Perhaps one day I shall tell you all the details, but not today. Now, I will tell you the outcome, which is that Jean lives with his father and sometimes he stays with us so that my mother and myself can keep close to him. We all want Jean to know that we are part of his family. It helps him to feel secure.'

He clung to her hand. 'But don't think that Jean isn't happy with his father because that wouldn't be true. His father adores him and has adjusted his work and life to being a single parent. We are very fond of him and try to help whenever we can.'

'So he is here for the week or . . . '

'No, it was just for today. His father had business in the area and it was a good opportunity to drop Jean in to see us. This often happens.'

'I see,' she said softly.

'If you had been here at dinner, you would have met my brother-in-law and also . . . '

She leaned forward with her head in

her hands. 'What must you think of me?' she muttered. 'But it was the very last thing I would have thought of.'

He took her hands away from her face and kept hold of them. 'You didn't know, how could you? Of course, I didn't know he was coming either until the last minute and had no idea that you'd seen him arrive, I couldn't imagine why you'd changed so much since this morning. I couldn't believe it when I heard you had gone to the village and not kept our arrangement.'

'I had to keep out of your way while I tried to deal with what I thought was happening.'

'I heard you were with Pierrre and I also jumped to the wrong conclusions and assumed you were spending the evening with him. I know that he is very attractive to women.'

'This morning,' she choked knowing that at any moment, she would cry. 'It all seems so long ago.'

'I couldn't warn you about the visit because it was only just before breakfast that my mother was telephoned with the arrangements.'

She thought back over the morning. 'Yes, I felt something was happening at breakfast, but nobody mentioned anything to me.'

'No, cherie, I understand. But she probably couldn't. It is a very sad story and she keeps her feelings hidden. But it is so bittersweet when her grandson arrives. It is something she tries to hide and so can appear a little off hand. He is so like her daughter in his way. It is often too much for her.'

'Oh Gerrard, I wasn't criticising her, please don't think that. It was just a different atmosphere and of course this is family business which doesn't include me.'

He stopped holding her hands and let his own travel in a gentle caressing motion around her wrists and then along both arms until he reached her shoulders when he pulled her towards him, holding her close.

'Cherie,' he whispered into her hair.

'We must put this behind us and start again.'

Her relief was overwhelming and she realised her true feelings for this man. Relief that all her doubts had been explained away mingled with the exquisite pleasure of being in his arms.

He stroked her hair and murmured endearments in an enchanting mix of French and English. She had never felt so utterly content, but equally the raw emotions of the day had drained her and left her drowsy.

'I couldn't bear to think of you with Pierre,' he said suddenly.

She twisted slightly so that she could look at him. 'Really,' she questioned archly, 'and why is that?'

His blue eyes were bright under his dark brows and his reply left her breathless and was all she had hoped.

'Because, cherie, I love you. I didn't realise how much until you didn't appear at dinner. The thought of you with Pierre made me madly jealous.' She felt his body tense. 'If I had seen him I'm sure I would have hit him.'

'Come,' she teased, 'that's not very civilised.'

'Ah, cherie, you forget that I am half French and we are a very volatile nation.'

'Oh Gerrard,' she murmured, 'this is all wrong I should never have allowed myself to be involved with you. I kept telling myself I was here to do a job and that was all, but you were always on my mind.'

'Surely you guessed how I felt about you.'

'Yes sometimes, but other times I wondered if you were using me to check up on Robert.'

'That was never the reason, but it was an excuse to be alone with you to talk about it. Poor Robert, I think I did him a great injustice for I'm sure he is only interested in my mother.'

'Yes that's right. He as good as told me.'

'But why are we wasting time talking about other people.' He bent his head and brushed her lips with his own. Feather-light but firm, they brushed again and again, starting at the corner of her mouth as soft as a butterfly wing. Tantalising and teasing they nearly drove her out of her mind.

Her world was full of his lips against her own, of his body close to hers and the fragrance of the soft French night which wafted in through the window and was all around them.

'Hannah.'

She loved the way he said her name. 'Yes.'

But he didn't answer, but deepened the kiss and drew her close and even closer while his hands caressed the back of her light T-shirt and she could feel their warmth on her back.

'Hannah.' He said again.

She tried to sit up straighter and pulling away, she shook her head. What she was doing was not right. There was a time and a place for everything and this was not the right time.

She must finish her job first because

this man had so much power to influence her and she knew she must keep him at arms length for a few more days.

'Hannah, do you love me?' he asked.

'Please understand, Gerrard. This is very difficult, so please help me. You know why I am here and I must finish my work. It must come first.'

He frowned as he listened to her and then asked again. 'Hannah do you love me?' His voice dropped as though he was uncertain. 'Please Hannah, tell me if you love me.'

'I love you, Gerrard,' she said as she looked into his eyes. 'But the time is not right, can you wait while I finish the job I came to do.'

'I am not a patient man cherie, but yes, I can understand and I'm sure you must be almost finished by now. But promise me that there will be time for us and very soon.'

'Yes, I promise and no, it will not be very long until we have time for ourselves. But please will you go now,

Gerrard. It is hard for me to say this, but will you please leave me?'

He drew her back to him and gave her one last lingering kiss and then stood up. 'If I know you love me, I can wait.'

9

The old chateau creaked in the wind. Hannah lay awake listening to the unfamiliar sounds thinking it was hopeless to try to sleep as her mind was going over all the events of the last few days.

Gerrard, true to his word, had kept his distance, but his feelings were revealed in every glance they exchanged and there were always opportunities for him to touch her hand in passing.

These loving small gestures spurred her to finish her work in record time. And now at last it was complete apart from some general tidying up of her notes and pictures.

This evening she had typed what was thankfully the last batch of notes and filed them with the digital photographs which she'd run off on her small laptop computer. She stretched luxuriously, happy with the way everything was going.

A tree brushed against something outside. Then as she listened it sounded wrong and appeared that the noise was now coming from within the house and not outside after all.

She shut her eyes so she could concentrate better on the sound. It was like the noise of someone walking or rather creeping and the odd muffled sound now seemed to be above her head. It just has to be the wind she told herself and probably imagination. A reaction to all the hard work during the last few days.

The gallery was directly above her room so no-one would be up there at this time of night. But if there was someone up and around, it wasn't anything to do with her. Anyone had the right to be up if they couldn't sleep. She'd often got up for a warm drink when she'd been at home, but would never wander around this place at night for it was far too big and grand.

Wanting to get away from the odd sounds and her too fertile imagination, she pulled the duvet over her head. Tossing and turning, she thumped the pillows and then suddenly warm, pushed the duvet away from her head.

Her heart began to pound as she heard the noises again and this time she thought she caught a muffled exclamation. It was no good, she had to see what was going on even if the place was big and grand, she was going to find out what had disturbed her. There was definitely a person above her, surely no-one was ill! Perhaps her help was needed.

She was out of bed before she'd thought about it pulling on a light robe, but not stopping to put anything on her feet. She lightly closed her door and swiftly went along the corridor until she reached the staircase. It was here that she very nearly turned back for the stairs reared up into the darkness like a prehistoric monster. There was no way she could climb those stairs, no way at all.

Then taking deeps breaths, she stood trying to calm her racing pulse for now she was very frightened, but in spite of her fear, something urged her on. That something in her head forced her on to the first stair and then the next and so she made her way in the dark at first and then as she climbed nearer to the top, a cloud must have shifted for the moonlight came in through a high window.

What she saw was unbelievable, and smothering a gasp, she sank to her knees and tried to keep within the shadow, because standing in front of the tapestry were two figures.

One she was sure was Pierre and the other could have been the young man she saw with him in the village.

Pierre was holding on to the tapestry while the other man had something in his hand and appeared to be levering the side of the frame.

She was trapped, any noise and they would see her and what would they do? But she couldn't stay here because once they'd finished they would see her anyway when they came to the top of the stairs. Her heart pounded so much she could hear it in her head and her mouth dried with terror.

She thought quickly, and born of desperation an idea came to her. Perhaps, just perhaps she could gently slide backwards down the staircase without making a sound and then she could get help. What a stupid and impulsive fool she'd been to deal with this on her own.

Slithering down, she made her way slowly while hardly daring to breath. At the same time she listened for any noise above her that would signal she had been discovered. It was going better than she expected and she progressed steadily until she was about halfway.

If only she could reach the landing below she was confident that she could gain the sanctuary of her roof and then try to raise the alarm. What a fool she'd been to leave it. Common sense should have told her that if anything was going on she was unable to deal with it single handed.

Suddenly she grinned thinking that she must look like a worm or some kind of insect as she slipped down the stairs. She tried to see the funny side of it, but it didn't really work and she could feel the clamminess on her face and knew that she'd never, ever been so afraid, had never been aware of such fear.

Her wandering mind caused her to lose concentration and all at once she was out of control and instead of sliding gently and silently she was moving more quickly and bumping noisily as she went.

'Oh,' she gasped as every bump and knock felt like stones against her body in its light clothing. There was a sound of a man's voice from the gallery. Just a few gruff words in quick, guttural French which she couldn't make out. It wasn't Pierre, she was certain of that.

Thrusting out a foot she at last managed to stop her impending plunge and where once she was conscious of her thudding heart, she was now convinced that it had stopped working altogether. And then she couldn't breathe and realised that she was holding her breath.

Slowly she found that she was breathing again and stayed absolutely still. She'd been lucky and had not been discovered. Immediately she calmed down and gathered herself to continue her way in the darkness. The staircase which she usually bounded up so lightly, seemed endless.

She never knew which came first, the click or the shaft of torchlight which encircled her head.

There was a swift intake of breath and Pierre's voice said, ''annah,' with an expression that was both despairing and angry. 'Hannah,' he said it again and even managed the 'H' this time. Then another voice raised in anger stumbled over what he was saying.

It took a few seconds before she registered that she'd been discovered and had nothing to lose in standing up and rushing down the rest of the steps. But, her brain whirled, she must do more than that, she must wake the household, both to catch the culprits and for her own safety.

She must have people to help her. So she gathered up her skirts like an old-fashioned maiden and ran and as she ran she opened her mouth and screamed.

The terrible noise she made startled even herself and someone rushed past her giving her a shove as he ran. She fell against the ornate banister and felt the decoration leave their mark on her back. Somehow she knew one of them had gone and that it was not Pierre.

She lay half stunned for what she thought was a long time, but it was only minutes and Gerrard found her still hard against the balustrade where she was sobbing with both fear and pain.

'Cherie,' he whispered. 'What is happening here? Are you all right?' He studied her face and put his arms gently around her.

'The other man,' her voice shook. 'He's gone, he pushed me to one side, but I'm all right. But,' she didn't want to tell him this, 'Pierre, he is at the top of the gallery. I think they were after the tapestry.'

'Pierre?' He looked bewildered. 'Why would Pierre be involved in this? I thought it was just one man because someone rushed through the kitchen and out the back entrance. Almost immediately a car sped away so there was no point in me following. But why are you up here?'

She shook her head wildly and her long fair hair swayed from side to side. She was unable to speak and for a moment he held her close. 'I should have told you about Pierre, you see I saw him in the village with someone who the waiter said was shady and I . . . '

'Tell me later, cherie,' he obviously thought she'd had a blow on the head and was talking nonsense. 'I'm going up to him. Robert,' he turned to the American who had now joined them. 'Look after Hannah for me, please.'

She looked up vaguely not having heard Robert approach. 'Come Hannah,' he said, 'We'll leave Gerrard to deal with this. I think Anne is in the kitchen and making coffee. He put a fatherly arm around her trembling shoulders and gently led her down the remainder of the stairway. 'You must tell me what has happened.' He smiled. 'There was this blood curdling scream which woke everyone. A loud voice from quite a small person,' he teased.

'Pierre,' she said, shaking her head. 'I just can't believe he would be involved in something like this. It's terrible, truly awful.'

10

The kitchen was warm and snug and Anne looked unusually domesticated with the coffee pot in one hand and wearing a soft blue robe.

'Sit down, Hannah,' she looked keenly at the younger girl noting the pale tear-stained face which made her eyes seemed even darker. 'Can you tell us what happened.'

Sinking into a chair, she clasped her mug of coffee and wished that it was tea.

'I heard noises,' she told them, 'and I thought I should get up and investigate, but I wish I hadn't,' and she covered her face with her hands.

'Don't talk anymore,' Anne said, 'do you want to go back to bed?'

'No, oh, no,' her voice rose almost hysterically. 'I can't be alone, I'd rather be here with everyone.'

'Just sit quietly then, my dear and perhaps Robert will bring us all a cognac.' She smiled and took Hannah's hands and began to rub them. 'You are freezing cold and the brandy will warm you.'

It did, indeed, warm and relax her and she began to tell them the whole story right from her last walk with Pierre when he seemed so anxious about the tapestry staying in France. 'I think, that he thought Robert would take it to America to display in his gallery.'

'No, no,' the American explained. 'I thought nothing of the sort. The only thing I want to take away with me is Anne,' and he picked up her hand and gently raised it to his face.

All at once Hannah felt an outsider. Here were two people, not young, but that didn't matter, but so very much in love. Robert could never pass for French or even English, he was pure American for his open and frank face to the expensive dressing gown, tied at the waist.

Anne looked warmer and with her hair loose around her shoulders instead of her usual chignon, much younger and more vulnerable.

She hoped that they would be very happy together and the thought made her feel very alone.

Then she remembered the last evening in the village and told them about the person who was with Pierre and how uncomfortable Pierre had looked, and what the waiter had said about the other man.

'I should have told someone, I should have told Gerrard, but ... ' She stopped and realised that her mind was full of her discovered love with Gerrard and the episode of Pierre and the other man had slipped into the background.

'Don't worry, Hannah, you had nothing substantial to go on. We could not have done anything about Pierre.' He patted her shoulder. 'I think it is all falling into place,' Robert ran a hand across his grey hair. 'This was obviously planned and you, my dear, stumbled into it without realising what was going on.'

'What has happened to Gerrard?' She twisted the tie of her robe with agitated fingers, remembering how afraid she had been, alone on the staircase with the two men above her.

'Don't worry,' said Robert, 'I don't think much of Pierre's chances, Gerrard might be slim but he has a big height advantage and a more powerful build.'

'But to think that a friend could behave in such a way.'

'The French are very excitable my dear. They feel emotions very deeply and of course have a strong sense of patriotism. He probably thought he was doing it for the good of his country. But I don't like the sound of this other man. He was obviously the ring leader and I expect Pierre was easily led.'

Hannah leaned back wearily in her chair. Anne was taking it all in such a down to earth manner that she could hardly believe it. Perhaps, she thought, things like this happen in France all the time.

And then the door opened and Gerrard entered. She couldn't help herself as she left her chair and ran to him. 'Are you all right?' she cried. 'Where is Pierre?'

'Pierre has left us, I'm afraid for good.' He looked across at his mother. 'This changes things, Maman. We will have to make new plans for the chateau of course, we could never allow Pierre to be involved in them now.'

Hannah gasped as reality hit her and she came back to the real world. 'Does that mean that all my work is wasted, it has all been for nothing.' Then she stopped abruptly and said, 'Oh, I'm sorry, how selfish of me.'

'No, my child.' Anne glanced across at Robert. 'We will just have to alter our ideas, but tonight is not the right time. We are all exhausted and there will be time enough to talk and plan in the morning.'

She rose from the table, took her

coffee mug to the sink and looked at Robert. 'I think we'll leave these two young people alone. I think they have a lot to talk about, but our plans,' she looked at Robert, 'will wait until the morning.'

11

Once the door had closed, Gerrard placed his hand over hers on the table, and they sat like an old married couple both lost in their own thoughts. He sipped at his coffee and she thought that the smell of coffee and cognac would always remind her of this moment.

It was Hannah who broke the silence. 'You were gone a long time and I was becoming so worried about you although,' she tried a weak grin, 'Robert said you were more than a match for Pierre.' When Gerrard didn't answer she asked, 'What is going to happen to Pierre?'

'I had phone calls to make of course which took time, but Pierre has gone home. I thought he was a friend, but he will never come here again.'

'You must be very upset at his

treachery, but I can't help feeling that he is not really a bad person.'

'We spent time talking about it. I think he was very misled and hardly knew the other man or so he says. But I will probably be satisfied just to see the back of him. We wouldn't like the police too involved which means bad publicity for us and I have a certain sympathy for Pierre.'

'I feel so dreadfully guilty, Gerrard. I was trying to tell you when you found me on the staircase that I had seen Pierre with this man in the village. Although of course, I didn't know who he was, but,' she tried to smile, 'when I asked the waiter, he said he was a shady character.' Her eyes filled with tears, 'maybe if I said something, this could have been avoided.'

'No, I think it was going to happen so please, my love, don't blame yourself.'

'But when I was walking with Pierre, he said some strange things about the tapestry and that it should stay in France, but I never dreamt, I never thought . . . ' She was unable to carry on.

'Forget all that, because it would have happened anyway. But,' he looked at Hannah, 'you should rest now, cherie. Half the night has gone. Will you be able to sleep now?'

'Yes, now that you are here and I know it is all over.'

Gently he drew her to her feet and wrapped his arms around her. 'Thank goodness you weren't hurt, when I think of the other man pushing you, you could have overbalanced and fallen down the stairs.' His kiss was tender, and then hand in hand they left the room.

He left her at her bedroom door. 'Sleep well, my love.'

She leaned against him feeling desperately tired as all the strength drained from her and she began to shake uncontrollably.

Taking one look at her white face, he lifted her in his arms, moved to the bed and tucked her in like a child.

★ ★ ★

Her night was dreamless and it seemed almost immediately that someone was knocking at her door and she took a moment to decide where she was as the events of the previous night came rushing back to her mind. All at once she panicked as she remembered the happenings of the previous night. Who could be at her door and knocking so insistently?

'Mademoiselle,' a voice called and suddenly she recognised Marie.

'Come in,' she called, her voice full of relief, and Marie entered with a tray of croissants, coffee and juice. 'Oh Marie, thank you so much,' she said.

'Mr Gerrard is waiting for you in the hall,' she told her, 'but he said not to rush, he is happy to wait.'

There appeared to be no ill effects from the night except a slight bruising on her back and feeling better for her food and coffee she showered and dressed. Today she put on a full blue skirt with a soft white top and after brushing her hair, went downstairs in a happy frame of mind.

'Good morning,' she said feeling suddenly happy as she saw him waiting. Like herself he was dressed casually in blue jeans and a T-shirt.

'Come,' he took her hand and led her down the steps and away from the chateau. It was a perfect morning, crisply warm and with the events of the night behind her and walking beside the man she now knew she loved, the world was wonderful and nothing could make it more perfect.

Nothing, that was, until Gerrard stopped under an old and spreading tree and took her into his arms. 'When I saw you last night, hurt against the balustrade I realised how much you meant to me. I can never let you go Hannah. I think you are part of me now.'

His hands cupped her face and he continued, 'You have completed my life. I thought I had everything I wanted with my home and business and sometimes women who entered my life and left it just as quickly, but you Hannah, you are different. You belong with me here at the Chateau du Moulins.'

'I . . . er, I do,' she stuttered and then thought how ridiculous she sounded. Why couldn't she think of something more meaningful to say.

'Hannah, stay with me, marry me,' he held her away and looked into her eyes. 'Will you marry me and stay with me forever?'

She hesitated just long enough for her future life to flash before her eyes. What about her career? Where would they live would they really stay at the chateau and could she live under the same roof as Anne? What about Robert, where would he fit in?

More important could she leave her own parents and friends and country? Then she lost herself in his loving gaze and nothing more mattered. The important thing, the here and now of her life was this man who was holding her.

She nodded.

'Is that supposed to be 'yes',' he teased. 'Can you say it, Hannah? Can you say you'll marry me?'

She nodded again, unable to speak and then she smiled and opened her mouth. 'Yes, Gerrard, I'll marry you, yes, yes.'

'As much as I want you to myself, I think we have an announcement to make. There is some good champagne which we'll open for lunch with Anne and Robert and then this evening you and I will go out to dinner alone.'

'What will happen now that Pierre won't be here to run the hotel?' Then forgetting Pierre she gasped, 'What about my work, all the work I have done to publicise the chateau. What will the agency think if it is now not wanted.' She looked at him with wide, dark eyes. 'I don't think I've made a very good job of this. I've done everything wrong including falling in love with my employer.'

'We will discuss things with Anne and Robert over lunch because they have plans of their own which don't include the chateau.'

'Don't include it,' she repeated frowning. 'But it's Anne's home.'

'But she is happy to live somewhere else, especially with Robert. They are going to America, cherie, and it is up to me, well us, what happens now to the chateau.'

After the nightmare of the last night, she felt that she had fallen into a wonderful dream where she was indeed the fairy princess and mistress of a wonderful old French chateau.

'First, you mustn't worry about all the work you've done because what ever we decide to do, we will want the publicity and I know that you have done some excellent work.' He looked thoughtful, 'what do you think should happen to the place, Hannah? What ideas have you in the back of your mind?'

She spoke slowly, 'You know that right from the start I said it was a shame to shut away some of those old pieces of furniture and pictures?'

'Yes,' he answered, 'but at the same time you said it didn't seem right for them to be used by people who might have the money to stay there, but perhaps would not appreciate them and treat them with respect.'

'I know,' she said excitedly, 'but as I've been going round the rooms, writing descriptions and taking pictures, I daydreamed and often thought what a wonderful place it would make to run appreciation courses in art.'

He was silent while he took in what she was saying.

'Do you understand the type of thing I mean? If there is a course leader and class of students who love and appreciate art, they could stay at the chateau and each day they could look at objects of furniture or tapestry or just take a period of art history and discuss it.' Her voice rose excitedly now, 'I always thought it would be the ideal place and I'm sure you wouldn't have any trouble getting people to come here.'

'And all your work could still be used,' he joined in, 'for we would still need a brochure, but it would be aimed at a different clientele.'

'Exactly,' her voice was firm. 'That's exactly what I mean. What do you think?' She crossed her fingers behind her back thinking that this would be the perfect setting for people who had an interest in and love of art.

'I think it's a superb idea. I would keep my Paris business because it is quite lucrative, but could put a manager in to report to me. I think that would work well. And you and I,' he grinned at her, 'We could run this place, with help of course.' He picked her up and swung her round. 'It's a wonderful, wonderful idea and I can't wait to tell mother and Robert.'

'Yes,' she almost squealed, but didn't mention her bruises, 'I can see Robert recommending us and having students from America. It's going to work Gerrard, I just know that it is.'

'We'll need help, Marie couldn't do everything like she does now.'

'And we'll want tutors to take the classes. But it will work, I know it will.' They wandered back with their arms around each other, still talking and planning for a wonderful future.

12

Anne and Robert were in the library when they arrived back and taking one look at their glowing faces, Anne stood and kissed first Hannah and then Gerrard. 'I know you have some good news to tell me,' she said.

Hannah smiled at the older woman and then at Robert who looked completely bewildered.

'Can anyone tell me what's going on here,' he asked and had never sounded more American. 'You women seem to have a silent language of your own and we men are never allowed in on it.'

'I'm going to get the champagne,' Gerrard told him, 'and then you can congratulate Hannah and I, for we are going to be married.'

'My dear girl,' he hugged Hannah. 'I couldn't be more pleased to know that you are going to be part of the family.'

Then grinning he called after Gerrard, 'You better make that two, my boy, one might not be enough, and by the way, the second bottle is on me.'

Gerrard stopped abruptly. 'You mean it's official now at last?'

'Yes, your mother has consented to marry me and yes it is now official and we don't care how many people know.'

Hannah sat down abruptly. It was beginning to go over her head, all the excitement in one day and there were things she must do herself. She must telephone her parents, what a shock they would have. But she was sure they would love Gerrard and perhaps she could ask them to come over here.

Also the agency who had been so good to her, they would have to be told. Maybe she could freelance now and again for them if there were other jobs around here.

'Hannah, where are you, we're about to have a toast,' Robert thrust a cool glass of champagne into her hand and suddenly they were hugging and congratulating each other.

Later at lunch, a smiling Marie and Claude were invited to join them and so the afternoon went on in that typical French style of good wine, food and conversation while they talked about the plans the young couple had for the chateau.

'It will still be run as a hotel,' Gerrard told them, 'but for people who love and want to learn about art.'

'I think that will be quite perfect, quite perfect,' Anne's voice was slightly unsteady though whether with emotion or champagne, Hannah couldn't tell.

At last Hannah's own eyes became difficult to hold open, the broken night, the wonderful morning and the champagne had quite exhausted her.

Anne's face was also pale and she got up and stood close to Hannah. 'I think that you and I, my dear, could do with a well earned rest. We'll leave these men to drink the last of the wine while we go to our rooms.'

Gratefully Hannah followed Anne from the room, just hesitating a moment as she felt Gerrard squeeze her hand.

The door closed on the men and Hannah felt suddenly vulnerable. Anne had said very little during their discussions and of course it could be possible that she didn't like any of their ideas. Although she'd been on friendly terms, she hadn't felt close to Anne during her stay and this woman was about to become her mother-in-law. Suddenly she wished that Gerrard was here giving her his support.

Her steps hesitated as she wondered if she should speak to Anne and ask right out if she approved of what they were going to do for, after all, she was the rightful owner of the chateau.

But she need not have worried, for Anne stopped at the foot of the stairs and placing her hand on the balustrade, looked directly at Hannah and said, 'I'm very happy to leave my lovely chateau in the hands of you and Gerrard.'

Hannah gave a little gasp of pure relief and happiness, it was wonderful that Gerrard's mother was on their side.

Anne continued, 'he, of course, thinks it the most wonderful building anyone could ever wish to see and you my dear, I know, appreciate its qualities.'

Hannah opened her mouth to acknowledge this but Anne hadn't finished what she had to say. 'I have watched you work and have seen some of the notes and pictures that you have and they tell me that you too are falling under its spell.'

'I love the place,' Hannah at last managed to speak, 'the more I've researched its contents and absorbed the atmosphere, I've come under a magic spell. But how can you bear to leave it?'

'Robert, he is the reason and knowing it will be in good hands and,' she shook her dark hair slightly, 'hopefully generating enough money to maintain itself.'

They started to climb the stairs, still talking. 'Robert has a gallery, as you know, so I shall still be involved in the art world and maybe we can recommend people to come here.'

'We've already thought of that.' Hannah laughed.

Anne looked momentarily sad. 'The one thing that has cast a shadow is this business of Pierre. He was becoming like one of the family and I was fond of him.'

'Don't think about it, Anne, perhaps he was just easily led and somewhat mixed up.'

'You're right, of course,' said Anne and reaching the landing they went their separate ways.

* * *

When Hannah reached her room, she was too excited to rest and paced around, looking at her notes and wondering when to telephone her parents. She must be careful and not alarm them with mentioning the happenings of the previous night. Also it would be good if Gerrard could speak to them himself.

Eventually, she could keep her secret no longer and bursting with happiness, she telephoned them and told them she was going to be married.

Although they were pleased for her, they wanted to meet this man their daughter was going to marry and she could read between the lines that they would not be happy until they had seen him. But they sent their love and wished her every happiness and asked if she had made any arrangements for a wedding.

Promising that Gerrard would also speak to them later in the day, she replaced the receiver and wondered how long an engagement they would have. Gerrard hadn't mentioned anything, but only asked her to marry him.

But that was enough, she hugged herself, that was surely enough.

Later that evening, in a very stylish restaurant, she said, 'My parents loved you, I'm sure they did.'

'But I only spoke to them, they haven't seen me, but when I mentioned that I would travel back with you when you leave, so that I can meet them, they were very pleased.'

'But you must have made a very good impression. My mother prides herself that she can tell a person's character by their voice and what they say.' She smiled. 'And I think she was very taken with you.'

'So when are you going to marry me?' he asked leaning towards her across the table.

Then they were interrupted with the arrival of their main course. The warm smell of herbs drifted up from her plate and she knew that the food was going to be wonderful, as wonderful as Gerrard looking at her, his bright blue eyes full of love.

'When would you like me to marry you?' she asked with a teasing lilt to her voice.

'How about when we go to England to hand over the publicity you've done, we could see your parents and ask them where they would like their daughter to be married.'

'How thoughtful of you, Gerrard. Although I have this feeling that you would like to be married here.'

'I think it would be wonderful to be married here, but it is the bride's choice and also her parents', so whatever you chose, I will be happy to agree.' Ignoring the plates of food in front of them, he took both her hands, 'the only important thing is that you marry me and soon, my wonderful Hannah.'

'Do you think our mothers will like each other because if they do, I can't think of a lovelier setting for a wedding than the Chateau du Moulins.'

His smile was wide and happy. 'I'm sure they will and they could have a wonderful time sharing the arrange-ments, and Mother will be delighted to see us married before her and Robert go to America.'

They stayed holding hands, their food forgotten, while they were both lost in their dreams.

Then Gerrard brought her hands to his mouth and kissed them. 'It would be nice to be married at the chateau, but where ever it is, the important thing is that you marry me. My lovely Hannah, nothing else really matters than that we will be together.'

The End.

We do hope that you have enjoyed reading this large print book.

Did you know that all of our titles are available for purchase?

We publish a wide range of high quality large print books including:
Romances, Mysteries, Classics
General Fiction
Non Fiction and Westerns

Special interest titles available in large print are:
The Little Oxford Dictionary
Music Book, Song Book
Hymn Book, Service Book

Also available from us courtesy of Oxford University Press:
Young Readers' Dictionary
(large print edition)
Young Readers' Thesaurus
(large print edition)

For further information or a free brochure, please contact us at:
Ulverscroft Large Print Books Ltd.,
The Green, Bradgate Road, Anstey,
Leicester, LE7 7FU, England.
Tel: (00 44) **0116 236 4325**
Fax: (00 44) **0116 234 0205**

THE FOOLISH HEART

Patricia Robins

Mary Bradbourne's aunt brought her up after her parents died. When she was ten, her aunt had a son, Jackie, who was left with a mental disability as the result of an accident. Unselfish and affectionate, Mary dedicated her life to caring for him. But when she meets Dr. Paul Deal and falls in love with him she faces a dilemma. How will she be able to care for her cousin, when she knows she must follow her heart?